THE CHRISTMAS JOURNALIST

L.A. CHANDLAR

LA CHANDLAR is an author and motivational speaker. In addition to her latest novel, *The Christmas Journalist*, Laurie's historical fiction and mystery series has a fresh take on 1930s New York City. Her *Fight to Keep Creativity Alive* series focuses on creativity and how it helps us work, play and live more fully. Laurie lives in New York City with her family.

www.LAChandlar.com

Cover design by Dave Gnojek

Author photograph by Britt Dyer

Edited by Amy E. Bennett

ISBN 978-0-9892360-4-1 (Trade Paperback)

ISBN 978-0-9892360-5-8 (Digital Book)

Printed in the United States of America

A Note from the Author

Historical fiction has always been one of my favorite genres. Too often we learn about history in pockets, an event at a time. We don't get a good appreciation for all that was going on at that time and what it was like to live in a particular place or in a particular era. Christmas has meant a lot to me personally, and I am fascinated by the history behind Christmas traditions. I wondered about what made these events happen. These weren't just events, they were people. So I took artistic license in thinking about the possibilities behind the lives of these amazing people. How did they get the idea? What might have triggered their inclination to throw a piece of gold into a stocking, write a poem, set up a Christmas tree? What could the backstory of their life have been? History books don't share some of that good stuff with us. So I hope these stories give you a glimpse into what *could* have happened, so that you enjoy the fullness of those traditions even more. This is a work of fiction, discrepancies with historical facts are due to artistic license in portraying the humanity behind the events. Any similarities to real people and real events are coincidence, although cameo appearances by real-life people are portrayed. If you like the stories of these people and these times, I've listed my sources in the bibliography for further reading.

CHAPTER 1

Jane Smith. A fantastically average name that goes splendidly with an ordinary life. I make up a full-house of unremarkable names. Marge is my mother, Pat is my father (not even Patrick), my sister Jennifer, and my brother Jim. I'm not a plain Jane; I think I'm pretty cute personally. And modest. Obviously. But everything else is… predictable. Don't get me wrong, my life is fine; I'm not unhappy. I especially like my job. However, I'm just not sure *fine* is good enough.

When BuzzFeed quizzes ask about the color that represents your life, I have long since quit searching for interest and sparkle because every time hope reared its head that perhaps there was some gold in the midst of the mundane…I get the answer: Brown. Brown is my color. Fabulous.

I'm from a small suburb of Chicago. I own a Chevy. I can't sing or dance or paint. I always feel like I'm looking for something; like life itself is missing an important piece of the puzzle. It's not romance, either. I've had a decent amount of romance, but I think it's deeper than that. It could be just a symptom of being a journalist. We are always hunting. Always searching.

"Jane!" murmured my mother, trying hard to get my attention but murmuring is about as loud as she gets.

"Mm?" I answered as I pushed around the mashed potatoes, disappointed that I forgot to surreptitiously add salt to the batch before it was plated. My parents were certain salt and sugar would "be the end of us" one day, so they kept careful watch over the white divinities that helped all humanity to actually enjoy their sustenance. I've had amazing mashed potatoes before. But somehow, my mom made the lowly potato even lowlier. It was like she added a spice that actually took away flavor. How is that possible? Don't even get me started on the Salisbury steak (ground beef with no seasoning and no gravy, cooked to oblivion to ensure that no germs – and probably no nutrients – had a chance).

"Your sister Jennifer," she began, because it's good to name her to differentiate between my other sister. Oh wait, I only have the one. "…called me today. She's really upset about her job."

"What do you mean? I thought things were going better," I said, as I swept a piece of steak off my plate into my napkin. My sleight-of-hand was getting pretty impressive at these weekly family dinners.

"Oh the agency is fine. It's just not what she wants, I guess."

"But I thought that this was The One. Wasn't she happy with the location, the people and the pay?" It was hard to keep up with my sister. In some respects, you'd think my parents would inspire jobs that had a typically boring title. But my sister had quite an exciting career in advertising, traveling all over the world. I never understood how someone could take an interesting life and actually make it dull. We're a talented lot, us Smiths.

"Oh, I'm sure she'll be fine. Eventually," said Mom. I love my mom, but in the funny way you love an old, beat-up pair of slippers. I've come to grips with the fact that we'll never have a relationship that grows; where I'll eventually see that she was the wind beneath my wings and that we're best friends after all. It's just not how we work. We can't seem to talk about anything important and she doesn't understand why I think life is a bit drowsy. You see, she's okay with drowsy. I have to appreciate my slippers for what they are and make the most of it. "You know, Jane, you really should be looking for a more stable job. This writing you do for the interweb is just not... oh... stable enough."

"You said stable twice."

"Well I meant it twice as much. You should go looking for a real writing job at like a magazine or something."

"I do work for a magazine."

"I mean a real one."

"Just because my magazine is an online magazine, doesn't mean it's less real. And besides, my articles get uploaded to other mainstream magazines too."

"Can I hold your 'real' magazine in my hands and flip the pages? No."

"If you had an iPad you could."

"I don't need an eye patch. My eyes are just fine. What does that have to do with anything anyway?" I looked to my father for help. Jim snickered when he saw my glance at

Dad. Dad stared right at me but with an opaque look in his faded eyes. He usually reads the newspaper 24/7. I think it was so that he didn't have to cope with the family. The opaque look in his eyes made me think he was still with the paper in spirit.

Jim kicked my shins under the table. He was my only salvation.

"Well I have an eye patch and I love reading your articles, Jane." Jim was the oldest. And he was constantly keeping me guessing. He was an enigma with his shorter than average height, slight paunch and balding head. He worked in a cubicle-filled beige office that was reminiscent of Dunder Mifflin minus Michael Scott (darn it). I honestly can't remember what exactly he does. But this is the thing: he's the one who's the happiest of us all. And the most interesting. He does interesting things outside of work like biking and photography and twice he's gone skydiving. He won't touch ice skates or skis because he has this theory that we Smiths shouldn't strap things to our feet. But even at his job, he likes it. It's fun and interesting to him. Somehow he managed to get out from under the wet blanket my parents threw over everything exciting. I was still trying to figure out the trick.

"I especially liked the history piece you did on the Michigan Central Station in Detroit," he said. I felt a little frisson of joy hit my cheeks and paint them pink. That was my favorite article and it got the most critical acclaim. The same architectural firm, Warren and Wetmore, who built New York City's Grand Central Station, also built Michigan's. Right now, it's sitting derelict and a literal shell of what it used to be. It will take a miracle for anything to be done about it. Real estate gurus say that no one can buy it without expecting to lose money.

"Do you remember it, Mom?" I asked. "I wrote an article about how beautiful Michigan Grand Central was back in the day, and I interviewed old-timers who used to go there to take trains around the country. The article's pivotal point was where I laid out an idea to get a group of real estate moguls, non-profits, and artists to re-create the space. In typical models, the experts are right, investors will lose money. But what if historical landmark nonprofits joined together *with* the real estate moguls and the artists? What if the space was made into artist work spaces with housing options, and a hotel where the artists also invested with sweat-equity? If Jackie O. could rally to save Grand Central in 1975 when it was to be torn down in the name of Progress, then there could be a solution to save Michigan Central Station. It just has to be a different kind of solution." I was on a roll. I can really geek out on history. But… my mom's eyes had glazed over.

"Did you just yawn, Mom?"

"Oh sorry, Jane. What were you saying?"

Jimmy coughed over her. "It's a very well-done article, Jane. You should be proud," he said.

"Thanks Jimmy."

"Jim."

"Mm hm. Jimmy." I liked to call him Jimmy because he hated it so much. I long for a nickname. I just can't get one to stick.

Dad had somehow magically oozed over to the recliner to give in to the siren of the daily news. Mom was already cleaning the kitchen and my plate was thankfully taken away. If we'd had a dog I could've given him some of my dinner. My parents didn't believe in pets. Too dirty. Too much work. Too interesting, I suppose. I gratefully made my escape after I helped clean the kitchen.

The next morning, I drove to work in my Chevy sedan. I listened to the morning radio. God I hate the radio. Why do I listen to it every day? The commercials, the yelling morning announcers... I could almost shiver with the appalling rut that it is, but I can't seem to stop. Sometimes they say or do funny things, right? What if I missed something interesting?

I wish I could walk to work. Walking is much more interesting than driving. Lately, I've been getting the feeling that I was living for vacations. I didn't like that. I wanted my regular, everyday life to be infused with that kind of interest. Why did life have to feel drowsy? Not that I'm looking for constant amusement, either. I get it, every job has its mundane bits. I just can't put my finger on it.

Maybe my boredom with plain food, my plain name, plain parents and life, is why I ended up with a roommate named Bianca Shock. I'm dead serious; it's her real name. Bianca. Now that's a name you can sink your teeth into. Mix that with some Jane Smith and you have some pretty darn good mediocrity.

I pulled into the parking structure and walked over to my building and took the elevator to the fifth floor. My office featured an open plan with the only real office-with-walls reserved for my boss: R. Robert Robertson. Now, if that name has a certain ring to it, just wait… it gets better. You'll see.

Just as I had one foot in the glass door that separated our office from the others on our floor, "Smith!!!!" ripped through the air.

"Yes sir!" I pretended right along with him.

"Put your stuff down, and get into my office on the double," ordered Robertson.

"You got it." As I set down my bag and patted down my curly blond hair, making sure it wasn't going haywire, I made a mental note of the three stories that had been brewing in my mind and the main one I was in the middle of researching.

I needed to make a few calls to a group in Portland who started a new effort against human trafficking. A group at a local church joined up with police and began a genius idea of placing a couple of ads in papers that would draw out those likely to be involved with trafficking. When they called, a trained person with the police would say something along the lines of, "Thank you for responding to this ad. This is the police. We now have your number and will be monitoring your activity with any and all under-age persons of interest." They'd go on to offer help with sexual addiction, and other issues, and they now had a unique phone number to run against the phone numbers of other offenders. Within months, they had thousands of unique numbers and after one year, the numbers of trafficking incidents had gone down drastically. In fact, a company that monitors trafficking across the country couldn't figure out why there was this strange blip on their graphs of extremely low trafficking activity that happened to be in Portland. Right when this system took shape.

As you can see I was excited about this and had to finish up some final stats and two minor interviews. I was poring over these thoughts and to-dos as I walked into Robertson's office.

"Smith!" he barked, making me jump. "I have an idea." Oh no. "I want you to drop everything and I want you to do a history story – a sort of documentary – on Christmas, yes Christmas."

"What? But I'm already on this trafficking story out of Portland–"

"Yes, yes, I know," he interrupted. "And finish that up on the double, but I want your butt on a plane to New York to find out everything. My assistant, Moxie, has started gathering articles and a surprising number of events happen in New York City. Just like the movies. The worlds-end disasters always happen there and once in a long while, San Francisco."

Completely befuddled, I breathlessly uttered, "Everything? What everything? What do you mean? Why?"

"Everything, Smith. Everything. Every historical tidbit and story on Christmas. Why the stockings. How the tree-thing began. What's up with Santa going down a chimney. Everything."

"Everything on Christmas."

"Open the safe and give Jane one of my own personal bars of milk chocolate! You got it. Now get the hell out of my building and shut the door." He grabbed a cigar – that he never lit – and stuck it in his mouth to signal the end of the discussion. Yes, Mr. R. Robert Robertson fancies himself the real-life version of J. Jonah Jameson of Spiderman. I don't know how he's gotten this far in the industry; it's quite amazing actually. Since he's extremely good at what he does, I assume this eccentricity is overlooked.

"Mr. Robertson. I do *not* want to be a Christmas Journalist!" I said defiantly.

"That's the spirit!" *Face palm.* It was extraordinary just how many of my conversations with him ended with a good ol' face palm.

"It's October."

"That's right! So you better get moving. I love nothing better than helping my fellow man! You'll be considered The Christmas Journalist. I can see it now! Good-bye."

Over his shoulder, I could see my friends holding their stomachs, they were laughing so hard. They'd obviously heard all this since Robertson was truly bellowing in Jameson style. And they must've seen my face. I hate Christmas. Loathe it. It can't get over with quick enough.

In a rare moment of stalwart form, I stood up and said firmly, "No. I hate Christmas. No, no, no, no. I will not be getting on a plane to New York City. I will not be The Christmas Journalist."

CHAPTER 2

"The weather in New York looks to be mild at about 55 degrees this sunny October morning. We'll be landing shortly at LaGuardia. Welcome to New York." Damn it. I'm The friggin' Christmas Journalist.

I had taken stock on the relatively short flight from Chicago to New York City. What exactly happened here to change my mind? I'll tell you what happened: I was railroaded into it and then my own sense of journalistic curiosity betrayed me.

I had finished up my article on the Portland story yesterday and as I was wrapping up, Robertson threw a few sheets of paper onto my desk as he walked by without a word.

I didn't even acknowledge those papers until I had hit SEND for my trafficking article to be sent to the editors. I needed to grab dinner before I could go any further. I hadn't eaten since breakfast but I'd worked my tail off getting that story completed. Robertson was on an office-wide rampage, throwing stories to each of us. He does this seasonally. Like the rainy season in the Amazon, it's a total deluge that has the capacity to wipe out entire villages. But in the end, it is a force of nature and therefore life. So we deal with it.

Yeah, well, whatever. I still hate Christmas. I don't mind the parties and the festivities. That's all good. I don't even mind the hubbub of gift-giving or the Christmas music that starts after Halloween (except the few diabolical songs:

Grandma Got Run Over by a Reindeer, I Want a Hippopotamus for Christmas, and of course *All I Want for Christmas is My Two Front Teeth*. Shoot me now). I'm not a typical Scrooge. But it's just... It's just not all it's cracked up to be, I guess. And that lets me down more than anything. There's something unsatisfying about it all and it's just not worth the effort.

I slung my leather bag over my shoulder, tied the belt of my black wool coat, and admired my new black knee-high boots. I stuck my red hat on my head, smoothed my curls that were trying to make a break for it, grabbed the few papers from Robertson, and stomped out the door of my nearly empty office.

I walked a few blocks across the cold sidewalks to find one of my favorite places. The wind from the lake was making the air feel cooler these days, giving us glimpses of the winter to come. It was late October, but there were signs of Christmas appearing. For cryin' out loud, there were signs of Christmas pretty much after the stores were done with their back-to-school sales.

I opened the door of The Library and immediately felt less like a curmudgeon. The Library is not a library, but a sort of cool coffee house and lounge. The walls are indeed lined with bookshelves, but it's more like an English library mixed with a pub with more wine than Guinness. I found one of the corner wing back chairs and sat down with a pleased smile as I crossed my legs and waved hello to a waiter who had become a friend of mine. He smiled and went right over to the bar and got the quartino of wine that I always ordered, the Montepulciano. I saw him wave to the kitchen staff with some kind of hand signal that I was pretty sure meant the tray of cheese, olives and bread that I like.

Caleb came over and sat in the chair next to me. "Hey Jane, how are ya?"

"Pretty good. I have to do some reading for a new story I was assigned," I said, rolling my eyes.

"Ha ha!" he laughed. "What, you don't like the story? You should see your face!"

I gave him a mock-angry look, trying not to laugh. "Yeah, well. I'm not thrilled with the idea."

"What is it, something boring? Like dust bunny evolution? The reasons socks get lost in the wash? What?"

I wrinkled my nose in disgust, "Christmas. Blech. History and stories about the traditions of Christmas. Unh, shoot me now," I said.

He bent over with a hand to his stomach, "Ha ha ha!"

"Cut it out."

"That's a great story! You'll have a blast. I bet there are some awesome things to discover that most of us know nothing about. You'll be fine. You'll be a great–"

"Don't say it!"

"–Christmas Journalist!" I can't believe he said it. He got up and kept ha-ha-ha-ing as he went to help some new customers that walked in.

"Hmph." Well maybe I am Scrooge. I took a generous sip of wine and then a deep breath. Alright. Let's get to it. I took out the papers from Robertson.

A few of the sheets looked like Wikipedia files and other general website information. There were also some hand-written notes, probably from Robertson's assistant, on the history of stockings, wreaths, candles, Christmas trees, etc. But then a different color and texture in the middle of the stack caught my eye. It was a little pack of three old pieces of folded vellum. The bottom corner of the three pages was turned the slightest bit up and the packet was hooked onto the corner of one of the white sheets. It looked old and fragile and I was a little annoyed that Robertson hadn't kept it more protected in an envelope. It was a letter written in a tiny script, as if squeezing every letter, every single thought onto the front and back of those thin sheets of paper.

Dear Willow,

The other guys are trying their best to stay positive and give the people back home something to count on. Something to give them hope. But you made me promise not to. You wanted the real truth because that's how we both have always been. I will give you the truth here. No matter what, at least you'll know I'm not holding anything back from you. Most importantly, I give you the truth so that you can see the stark contrast of what happened last night. My mind is still reeling that this could have happened. A bright shining light of promise and beauty right smack in the middle of horror. How can this be?

But first the horrors. I'm truly sorry to write this, I pray it won't give you nightmares, but if you don't really know, if you don't really understand a tiny bit of the depth of what and how we are fighting, how can we continue? How we can laugh together and really, truly laugh? It seems like we would be living two separate lives instead of one. I can't keep anything from those beautiful gray eyes of yours...

I needed to pause and put the letter down for a moment as I realized I had just at that second fallen a little bit in love with this man. I mean, wow. I sipped my wine and ate a bit of cheese as I tapped the side of my cheek, deep in thought. The date at the top was December 26, 1914. World War I, for certain, then. I'd heard a little about an amazing event around that time, but like a little child not wanting to ruin dessert by eating her dinner, I kept myself from dredging up what I remembered from history classes so I could enjoy this letter to the fullest, in the moment.

But who was this man who seemed so different? Even in America, there was a standard sense that you needed to keep a stiff upper lip and not really tell your loved ones just how bad things were because that was the thing to do. And who was this Willow? That's not a typical name for those days. Perhaps it was a term of endearment. Alright, back to business.

We are living in trenches that we've dug in the ground. It's so cold, there are rats, you can't even imagine the mud when it rains. Then come the shells, the gunfire, the relentless bombing. More digging, burying the dead, getting the wounded to the

15

*ambulances. We dig a few feet further. The enemy
pushes us back to the same god-forsaken trenches
we'd been in a few days before. We press on, men go
up and over to fight and most don't come back. The
worst times are when men get caught in the barbed
wire and are shot, but not to death. Their cries and
screams are seared into all our minds. Then more
mud, the cold, the dirty rations, the filth and constant
turmoil of wondering how long? How long can this
go on?*

*Then came a strange day. It's so hard to keep
track of days. They slip and slide around in my mind.
The fatigue and strain make it impossible to think of
the calendar let alone which exact day it is,
sometimes. But in the morning, I realized it was
Christmas Eve. A few of the guys managed to keep
hidden a few token things like a couple of cigars, a
few rum balls, one guy even brought out a small
bottle of scotch. I can't even imagine how he'd kept
that safe! From both bullets AND the other guys!
Everyone shared and it was a moment of peace. The
camaraderie is something fierce. There was no firing
that day. I wasn't sure if it had been planned, but on
our side, there were no shells being fired, no
directive for going up and over. Just as I got a hold
of the bottle of scotch for a second round, we heard
it. Singing. We all grabbed our rifles and planted
ourselves in position. But the singing kept coming in
soft waves over No Man's Land, floating down into
our pits of mud and filth. It was soft and eerie and
suddenly I recognized a refrain where the English*

words go, "…sleep in heavenly peace." The Germans were singing the Christmas carol Silent Night!

We all looked at each other in shock. Then the singing stopped. Nothing. And one voice, a couple trenches over, but ON OUR SIDE sang softly, then more strongly, "O, holy night, the stars are brightly shining, it is the night, of our dear Savior's birth…" Then hums along with his clear words, backed up by his earnest voice. I don't mind saying there were several of us wiping a tear away. But then, a guy named Bugby (of all things) grabbed his hat, and slowly raised his arm up above the trench. You NEVER do that. I saw a guy get his hand blown off once and another time, well, you don't need to know that, but something even more important to living got blown off. Several of us started to go towards Bugby and were hushing him and waving him down. But he got this weird look in his eyes and he shrugged and smiled. He kept going and pushed his whole body up and over the top! But nothing happened. Nothing happened! The voices all had stopped on both sides and I can imagine the skirmish going on in the German's trenches just like ours. And then – I'll never forget it – I heard voices. INTRODUCING EACH OTHER. Bugby was in No Man's Land and apparently meeting with a German.

I just about had a heart attack. But then, please forgive me, I poked my head up over, too. Sure enough, there were the two soldiers, not being able to speak in each other's language, but clearly communicating. I was up and over by now, smiling

*and tentatively looking at the three Germans now up
and over their trenches, who were also smiling and
coming toward us with a very noticeable lack of guns
pointing at us. I rubbed my eyes, certain I was
dreaming. More and more men on both sides started
coming out. I still had the bottle of scotch in my hand
and I turned back to see the guy who had given it to
us. There was only about a fourth of the bottle left,
but plenty to share. I nodded at the bottle and then at
the Germans. He looked like a deer in the headlights,
but he nodded the affirmative: I could share it with
our enemies. So far only talking had taken place, with
one hand holding the bottle, I looked at the closest
German and nodded at the bottle as I stretched out
my hand – the universal sign of the hand shake. We
locked eyes and boy, did I see a lot in those eyes. I'm
sure the feeling was mutual. Something released in
the German's eyes at that moment, and his right arm
came out and grasped mine. I gave him the bottle for
a drink. We didn't try to say anything, but together
we looked around us. Little groups were forming all
over the place. Things were being traded, buttons cut
off and swapped. The rare chocolate bar here and
there divvied up. Off to the side there was even a
game of football starting up. One of the craziest
things I saw was one of our guys who was a barber in
regular life. He had his clippers out and one of the
Germans with unusually long hair was kneeling down
on the ground as our barber clipped his hair for him.*

*I'll never forget those few hours as long as I live.
It was a miracle, Willow. After living in the trenches*

– and I've not yet mentioned the absolute mental challenge through the monotony of it all – to see this piece of magic happen was simply of another world. I am a lucky man to get to be part of it. Franz and I gave each other one last handshake as the thoughts that we'd be shooting at each other tomorrow were most certainly running through both our minds. Those eyes that I had seen so much in, looked into mine one more time. He took his hand out of his pocket and handed me

Handed me what? I flipped the page over and over oddly thinking that this would make a new page appear out of thin air. There had to be more! I had to know what he handed him and how the letter ended! I wanted to hear more true words from this incredible man. I looked carefully through the stack of white paper, I patted through my bag in a panic, and I even looked under my chair in case it had fallen out.

"Whoa whoa! You look like you're about to toss the joint!" said a smirking Caleb.

Caught with the seat cushion in my hands, I smiled self-consciously and slowly lowered it back into position. "Oh no, no, no. Nuthin' to see here."

"Mm hm. Right. And I'm not paying off $50k of school loans. What else you got?"

"Alright, you got me. I think I might have lost an important part of an old letter. It just has to be here!" I was feeling an exquisite desperation to find the end of that incredible letter. I needed to know what that German handed him and I most definitely needed to know his name. I didn't even know his name! The letter wasn't in an envelope and the only clue was the enigmatic name of Willow. At the top it did have a street address and it was in New York. Assuming Willow was in her 20s when the letter was written, she'd be approximately 120 years old. Definitely not still around, but I at least had a starting point.

Three things came together to catapult me to Gotham. One, the missing piece of the letter. Two, the curious idea that maybe R. Robert Robertson knew I'd be seduced by the history and had planted this partial tasty tidbit on purpose. And lastly, my mother.

If only the phone call hadn't been a typical example of our relationship. But it was. "Mom! I have to fly out to New York City, I got an assign—"

"Blech! New York City!" she cut in. "Why in the world would anyone want to go there? You just tell that boss of yours that you are not going, that that city would eat you alive."

The *what* would do *what*? "Mom, I want to go."

"Don't be ridiculous. You have no business going there. Just finish up whatever little story you're working on now, and I'm sure a better story will come along. One that suits you better." It's nice to be understood so well by the woman who raised you.

At the end of her sentence, I could tell she'd turned her head to Dad and was murmuring in her marshmallowy voice, "Pat, don't you dare put salt on your meatloaf. Oh, did you get the milk and butter at the store? Oh good. Yeah,

I need it for breakfast tomorrow. Sorry, Jane. Anyway, what were you saying?"

It wasn't even that I minded her getting distracted with my dad's felonious salting; it was that she forgot what we were talking about. I toyed with the idea of telling her I was running away with a Pope impersonator and that we'd live happily-ever-after in Vegas since I'd be joining Cirque de Soleil. Before I could try anything fun, she said, "Oh! And by the way, I started my Christmas shopping! Did you?"

I booked the flight then and there. Most satisfyingly, right after I booked it, I got a text from my brother Jim: GO. TO. NEW YORK.

CHAPTER 3

The feeling of excitement grew as I took a cab from my hotel to the Upper East Side, ate lunch at a local diner nearby, and walked around the city. I adore Chicago, but I think people are right when they say New York City has an energy all its own. There is this vibe that bustles you along, not in a pushy, obnoxious way, but in a way that makes you want to get out and be in it, be part of it.

I was smiling as I turned corners or looked into the windows of restaurants. There was a conspicuous lack of drowsiness. Sometimes at home I'd feel so lethargic as I drove to work every day, met with the same friends, avoided spending time with my parents… But here I was wide awake and in spite of the homeless people dotted here and there on the corners, the trash that overflowed many of the trash receptacles, and the suspicious puddles from rain that had a greenish hue, there was something wonderful in the air. All the creativity of fashion, restaurants, shops, museums, and different kinds of career possibilities, gave the atmosphere a sense of hope and adventure. You never really did know exactly what would be coming around the corner.

I found myself ringing the bell of 121 East 83rd Street. It was a charming white townhouse tucked into a corner, framed by another townhouse on the right and a storefront on the left. So instead of a straight front, parallel with the sidewalk, it fit into the corner and created a wonderful and welcoming angle. There were window boxes on all the windows of its four stories, flanked by black shutters and a staircase heading from the sidewalk to the front door. On the first floor was a kitchen and you could see its golden light glowing out onto the sidewalk. For the fall season, orange and yellow mums mixed with straw, miniature pumpkins, and red berries overflowed from the window boxes. I wanted to go and explore that house just about as much as I wanted to find Willow's family and that letter.

It seemed like the white townhouse was beckoning to me, so I felt like an old friend as I bounded up those steps. It wasn't until after I rang the doorbell that the panic set in. Wait, wait, wait, I was about to *what*? What was I going to say?

The door opened and a man a little older than myself, probably early thirties, greeted me with an open smile, sparkling eyes, and a five o'clock shadow to die for.

"Can I help you?" God, yes.

"Uh, actually, I hope so." I shook my head just a tiny bit to clear the cobwebs and felt the curls of my hair bounce around my face. It was pretty cold, so I had a hat on and my bangs were about touching my eyelashes. "My name is Jane Smith from Chicago Magazine. I specialize in historical pieces and I'm doing an article on the history of Christmas traditions." His open smile had closed a little as I was speaking and I wanted so badly to make that come back. Maybe I'm not the only one who hates Christmas. His glittering eyes had dulled, too. He let a long pause plant itself between us after I finished my sentence.

"Let me make myself crystal clear. Whoever you are, I have no idea how you found this address or what kind of story you could possibly be writing but I can guarantee this hokey Christmas deal is not the real thing." His hand was shaking a tiny bit and a sheen of sweat started to form on his forehead as he brushed his dark brown hair back from his face. His lovely, lovely face. "Do you hear me?" I guess I forgot to look intimidated as I was admiring his fine self.

"Yeah. Absolutely. I hear you. But I can assure you, I truly am writing a Christmas piece and for cryin' out loud I'm not even sure you're the person I'm looking for." Yes, I'm sure. I'm really sure I'm looking for you.

"Well, uh, well. Who are you looking for?" he asked.

"She'd be long gone, but I'm hoping to find her family." He stiffened his back and his eyes darted down to the left and then back up to mine. I went on, "The only thing I have on her is this address and that her name is Willow."

At that he pursed his lips then said through his teeth, "Don't come back. Ever." And he slammed the door shut.

Completely undeterred – this can happen a lot to journalists – I casually walked down to the bottom of the steps and leaned back against the railing. I took out my phone from my messenger bag and tapped my chin. I crossed my knee-high black boots at the ankle and ruminated a bit. *Touchy touchy*. Boy had I struck a nerve! He clearly hadn't had any experience with reporters because that's exactly the kind of response we dream about getting. Kinda like waving a red flag at a bull. It means there's a good story here. I never give up on a good story.

I sent a quick email to Robertson's assistant, Moxie, to ask for some help with Willow and the past of this interesting man. I mean, this man's family. I walked over to Third Avenue to a little place called the Luncheonette that looked like it had been there since the 1920s. I took a small booth and ordered a hot cocoa and some French fries. It's a regular treat for me. Think Wendy's Frosty with fries in a hot version. Honestly, *Moxie*? The research assistant's name is Moxie. I am surrounded by name-whores.

I needed to think more about this enigmatic, good-looking man at the townhouse of my dreams. In the meantime, I would follow up on other intriguing parts of the Christmas history. I'd have to wait on the Santa Claus aspect. I had a couple of ideas of where I wanted to take that part of the story, but I'd really have to gird my loins, so to speak. Mine was a long history with Santa. My parents never believed in telling us kids about Santa. I got to really enjoy the extra fun role of killjoy as I unknowingly told a bunch of kids there was no Santa Claus. I was so popular.

Sure, we did Christmas trees and presents, but there was no jolly old Saint Nick who magically sent us presents. My parents were of the ilk that you shouldn't lie to your children and education was first. I guess that's fine. But there was always something missing in our celebrations, I think. What was it? We always appreciated the toys and the thoughts that went in to the gift giving. But why all the hype? Why all the stuff that you only do at Christmas? Why did it make people feel special? Wasn't it just a glorified way to be the over-the-top consumers that Americans are supposed to be? But why would the lack of Santa make me feel funny? Like something was missing? Maybe that magic of Santa represented more than just one of our cultural mores. Maybe.

Anyway, that was far too deep for me to wrap my mind around today. I was hoping Moxie could hook me up with a few people to go along with the ideas that I had for this project. There were an unusual amount of Christmas events that all came together in New York City; Robertson was certainly correct about that. I was definitely in the right place. In fact, my phone buzzed and Moxie had already gotten me a phone number to call for one particular tradition I was interested in. However, maybe I was in exactly the right place even more than I thought because as I looked up, Handsome Angry Man walked into the Luncheonette.

I popped another French fry into my mouth and watched him. Maybe he wouldn't see me. Nope. He saw me all right. Looked me right in the eye after he ordered something from the gal behind the soda counter. He walked toward me. All six foot two or so of him, with his sharp gray wool coat with an open collar that revealed some of the dark blue shirt beneath. His snazzy loafers clicked on the black and white tile floor.

He stopped right at my table and stood there.

I put my hands up in mock surrender. "I didn't come back. Just like you requested so nicely," I said to the unspoken challenge in his eyes. He squinted a bit like he was analyzing me, or considering the different responses possible.

"No, you didn't. But I did see you waiting at the bottom of the stairs. I got the distinct impression that I handled the situation completely wrong." I raised an eyebrow at him and tried to hide a smile.

"Yeah. You couldn't have acted more seductively to a reporter."

"Seductively?" he asked.

"Mm hm. For future reference, the more mysterious and obstreperous you act with a journalist, the more they know beyond a doubt that there's a story."

"Obstreperous. Nice word."

"Thanks."

"May I?" he asked as he started to sit down at my booth before I could reply.

"Well, I don't know. Why should I let you sit in my booth?"

"Did you just dip your French fry in your hot cocoa?" he asked, not answering my question.

"Yep." I said as I popped the cocoa-fry in my mouth and smacked my lips.

He looked like he was at odds with himself. Half disgusted and half intrigued. I gave in, "Of course. Sit down." He had already been seated, but he had the decency to say, "Thank you."

His burger and fries came and he took his napkin and placed it on his lap. As he picked up his burger and took a big bite, I bluntly asked, "So what's the big family secret you're hiding?" If I thought he looked at odds with himself a second ago, it was nothing compared to now. I excel at the well-placed bombshell question. It's a fascinating study of the human response. His eyes went wide with shock that I could be so blunt, but then he tried to quickly hide the fact that there *was* something to hide, plus a little indignation and yep! At last, a tiny bit of humor that ended up winning the battle of emotions.

With his mouth full, he said, hardly opening his lips, "Hey!"

I started to crack up. "I know. I know. Low blow. You had it coming." I ate another fry and said to him, "You called my magazine."

"Wait. What? How did you know?"

"I contacted them first. I figured you'd follow up on my claim and I told them to text me when you called." Now glimmers of that open smile I liked so much started to really appear in force. I smiled in return. "Can I at least know your name? We can start there."

"Yes. I did call them and they verified your story, that you're The Christmas Journalist." Oh good God. It's starting to take. "I'm sorry I didn't believe you. And yes, my name is–"

"Wait! Let me guess. Everyone in my life lately has fantastically unique names."

"What do you mean?"

"Well, my roommate is Bianca Shock, my research assistant is Moxie, and I work for R. Robert Robertson."

"That sounds like Spider Man."

"You have no idea. Is your name Tristan?"

28

"No." He ate a few fries as I figured out my top ten list of fancy names.

"Stone or Fletcher?"

"No." He was starting to enjoy this.

"Good. Aiden? Seamus? Xander?"

"No, no, no. The hot cocoa French fry thing is really good?"

"Yes. Definitely. Dip away, I'm done with it. Blaise or ooh! I've got a good one, Gaige?"

"Nope!"

"God, please don't say your name is Jack."

"I like the name Jack," he said.

"But Jack and Jane could never hang out. It's just too much."

"True. You have a point. There are just some names that are destined to not work out. The alliteration is awful. Jack Black makes it work. But my friend Amy once dated a guy named Dave Namy. If she ever took his name, she'd be Amy Namy." He raised his eyebrows like he was saying *top that.* "Are you ready for my real name?"

"Yes. If you tell me the truth that you're digging the French fry, hot cocoa thing."

He rolled his eyes, "Alright, I admit it. I don't like it."

"Liar," I said, as I smirked.

"My name's Drew… Clompsburg. Andrew. But I go by Drew." Drew is by no means a Jane type name, but it's not exactly Grayson or Logan, either. *Clompsburg.* Remind me to never disparage my plain last name ever again.

"Alright, Drew Clompsburg. I'm enjoying this banter. But why did you come here? After your abrupt door-slam, and no, I'm not forgetting that…" I said in response to his self-deprecating grimace. "I figured you'd seen enough of me."

He stopped and paused in a significant kind of way and looked directly into my eyes. "No. I haven't seen enough of you." Did the room swerve a bit or something? I think I felt the room swoop a little.

I quickly went on, "So, as you know from calling my office, I'm working on an article about the history of Christmas traditions. I have some research and some leads; that's actually how I found you." His eyes narrowed a bit, like mine do when I'm linking a few juicy tidbits of a story into one big scoop. Hmm. What was going on behind that interesting face of his? I went on, "I want to finish it up as quickly as I can. I have other stories I have to work on," I lied.

"You're lying." What? "Why do you want to finish up this particular story so fast? And don't say it's because of the deadline from your editor. I can tell it's something else."

"How do you know that?" I asked extremely skeptically.

"You looked shifty when you said that. And you crinkled your nose like you smelled something unpleasant."

"Oh. Well. I mean, it's not a secret, I guess. I'm not a fan of Christmas."

"Oh come on! You looked all excited when you were grilling me at the house."

"Nope. I hate it, actually. I love history, so that part of all this is exciting to me, but not Christmas itself. December 26th can't come fast enough." That contemplative look came over him again. He was considering something. I wondered what that was all about. I noticed neither of us had brought up Willow. I knew her name was what caused him to slam the door on me. I needed to go slow and get him to trust me before I could bring her up again. Maybe he felt the same way.

"I get it. It's just surprising," he said. I smiled as he ate his last fry *after* he'd dipped it in hot chocolate. Again. "I don't like it either."

I coughed. "Be serious. Of course you do. Everyone loves Christmas."

"Nope. Don't like it."

"Why?" I asked accusingly, having never before come upon another one of my species.

"You first."

"Oh. Well, I don't know. My parents never really were into it. When I was five or so I remember asking my mom about Santa Claus because my cousins were really excited about his visit. She said it was a silly, stupid little legend people told their children to get them to behave well. That smart people didn't believe in Santa."

"That seems a bit callous to tell a kindergartner," he said.

"Yeah. My mom is… different. Think of a mix of Leonard Hofstadter's mother in Big Bang Theory and the muffled speaker on the phone in the Snoopy Thanksgiving special. You know, the muffled voice that means an adult is talking and it's boring compared to the adventures the kids are having. She's a wet blanket. Everything fun is either dangerous, silly or unhealthy."

I thought back to the day that she'd said that about Santa. I'd never really thought much about that exact moment. I remember it was snowing outside and the snowflakes were making beautiful drips along the windows. I loved it when the snow gathered around the corners of windows, reminding me of old fashioned Christmas cards where you could see a horse-drawn sleigh outside the frosty windowpanes. That day I'd wanted so badly to go out and make snow angels. But my mom said it was too late for me to go out to play, even though about a dozen other kids were outside in the first snowfall of the season. That was when I asked about Santa. It was not a good day.

He was nodding. "So your Christmases weren't exactly magical with her wet blanket, huh. How'd *that* make you feel?" he asked earnestly. Suddenly, I'd had quite enough of this conversation. I felt my face redden and I started to get my scarf out of my bag. I wanted to leave. "Whoa! Whoa! I didn't mean to make you mad."

"I'm not mad."

"Liar." He was right; I was *really* mad. But dang if that cute face didn't make me smile even when I didn't want to. I hate that.

"Bah!" I said like Scrooge, which made him laugh. "I'm not mad *now.* I guess I just don't like talking about it."

"Hmm. Keeping it a secret, are we?"

My eyes brightened and he caught my reaction. He'd slipped, knowing I'd hone in on the word secret. "Oh, it's not a secret like *some* people keep."

It was his turn to redden and look rather angry. I simply smirked at him, my eyes not leaving his for one second. It looked like he was battling within himself to try to be haughty and say something withering. But I like that sort of tension; I knew I'd win. I kept right on staring at him.

"You win," he said, throwing in the towel by tossing his napkin over his finished plate of food.

"Oh yeah. But for now," I said, taking a moment to consider his face with a tilt of my head, "you can keep your secret. Don't get me wrong, I want to know what's behind *all this*." I swirled my hand in his general direction. "But I have a little time. You never know, maybe you'll tell me your secret of your own accord. I can work wonders, you know."

"I can imagine."

Now y'see? The room did that swoopy thing again. I think he took that a little differently than I intended. Now he was the one smirking. Was it hot in here? I think it got hot in here.

Just as I was starting to have a really good time, he said, "But for now, I do have to call it a day. I have a few things I have to get to."

"Wait, wait, wait! You can't just leave! Will you help me with… this Christmas article?" I was still afraid to say Willow's name. I didn't want to ruin the moment.

"Yes, I will. I even have an idea for you." He'd already gotten his coat on and was walking away.

"You don't even know where I'm staying! How will you find me?"

"You're not the only one who can do a little sleuthing. I'll find you."

After I got my breath back and he had his hand on the door, I said, "Well, all right then." I heard him chuckle as he swung the door open with a clang and strode outside onto Third Avenue.

CHAPTER 4

As I walked over to Fifth Avenue and then south, I pondered our little snack time. Even though Drew was willing to lend a hand with the Christmas article, making it seem like he had nothing to hide along those lines, I knew beyond a doubt that Willow was someone he had a link to. I had a sneaking suspicion that their family would be an intriguing part to this story.

I still hated the thought of spending so much time on the topic of Christmas, when most of my years I spent dodging the issue from November to New Years. Then I could take a deep breath and enjoy the next 10 months or so. All the rigmarole of buying presents that no one wanted, so that eventually our family's show of generosity deteriorated into exchanging gift cards with a set limit of $20 – bring on the childlike squeal of anticipation! It had all the spontaneity and romance of doing my taxes. And if Santa was just a silly legend, why did people make all that effort to pretend and hide presents and even set out cookies? It seemed useless. I mean, I get the religious reasons for Christians celebrating the holiday, but it sure had a lot of "additives" that had nothing to do with the Christ-child being born. I guess it all comes down to consumerism. I guess it's logical.

But… I was shocked at the notion that hit me, walking alone down Fifth Avenue, in a city not my own, on a mission I didn't like: I was sad. The consumerism made sense, but even after all these years suppressing any emotion around those dates, and avoiding that holiday every way I could, I hadn't realized that I was so sad about it. I heard a saying once, something like, "Hope deferred makes the heart sick." Maybe I needed to chew on this a little. I'm The Christmas Journalist? I should have become The Christmas Therapist.

My first meeting was with a Rockefeller historian. When I think of Christmas, I always think of Rockefeller Plaza with the enormous Christmas tree. So I set up an appointment with someone who was supposed to know all about it. Since I'd never been to New York before, and girded with my trusty Google Maps, I had decided to walk the whole way there. I passed Tiffany's, the Disney store, Bergdorf's, about a hundred restaurants, and eventually came to St. Patrick's Cathedral and Rockefeller Center. I didn't have time to go into St. Patrick's yet, but I would do that later. I'd heard there was going to be a beautiful light display against Saks with giant snowflakes running up and down the building, while *Carol of the Bells* played throughout the plaza. The crowds after the lighting of the tree – at least on weekends – were supposed to be massive. Already, even in late October, I could see the preparations beginning.

I found my address and went up to the 26th floor. I was meeting with an elderly gentleman named William. I sat down on the other side of his desk and we got right down to business after a short introduction. No dilly-dallying here. I asked if I could take notes, and Billy, he'd surprisingly preferred, looked as if I was an idiot to think he'd expect anything less.

"Now!" barked Billy, surprising me so much I almost dropped my laptop. "Let's begin with a little on the history of Christmas trees." Billy was of medium build, probably well built as a young man. But his body had softened with age. His light gray hair was sparse, and his glasses only increased the intensity of his brown eyes. Boy, were they sharp. No mental dilapidation here. I felt like I was constantly under scrutiny and had to perform like a student at a military prep school. I resisted the urge to say, Sir! Yes, sir!

My fingers flew as he spilled out his veritable knowledge. "Well, the traditions of trees began with the Vikings. They would bring the evergreens indoors for the freshness and for the hope that those green branches signified. Even in the midst of almost total darkness in those far northern climates, in the middle of winter, these trees not only survived, they flourished." I nodded as he looked at me as if I wasn't typing enough. I tried not to roll my eyes.

"But the tradition of Christmas trees didn't come to America until Pennsylvania Germans brought it in the 1820s. Then they really took off when Queen Victoria, who married the German Prince Albert, had a tree in Windsor Castle in 1841." I hadn't known that. My face must've shown it, because he went on.

"Prince Albert also sent decorated Christmas trees to schools in Windsor and to local army barracks. Soon every home in Britain had a tree decorated with homemade crafts, candies, and candles. Queen Victoria and Prince Albert brought the tree into Windsor Castle on Christmas Eve and they would decorate it themselves. They would light the

37

candles and put gingerbread on the tree and then the children would be brought in."

When he took a breath, I asked, "So tell me a little about the Rockefeller tree."

"Well, the average height of the tree is 70-100 feet and has approximately 45,000 lights. The Swarovsky crystal star on top has 25,000 crystals and the entire star is over 3 meters across." I thought *we* had problems getting the star on top of the tree without killing ourselves.

"So did the Rockefellers have a plan for the tree from the beginning of the work on the plaza?" I asked.

Billy smiled. I think he'd been hoping I'd ask. His countenance altered as he relaxed a little. A contemplative smile played around on his lips, and I could see the little boy through the octogenarian. "Well, now that's a good story. Let's grab a cup of coffee and I'll tell you all about it."

His secretary came in with coffee and we decided to sit over in the lounge area of his office. I sat in the corner of an espresso leather couch and he crossed his legs in a large wing back chair. I think he was deciding how to go about the telling of a story that delighted him. This was really fun.

Fine. This assignment was getting better. I admit it.

"Well, Jane, it's a story that changed the history of Rockefeller Center. And as all good stories do, it changed the life of one man, as well. This is how it all started…"

CHAPTER 5

New York City
December 1931

The door slammed shut. A door slam means so many things. It can mean anger as it's slammed behind an argument. It can mean betrayal when it's slammed behind someone walking away from someone else. It can mean defiance as a teenager slams it shut because no one understands his life. It can even be funny like when a toddler closes it too hard and scares himself, but then he giggles with the delight of the surprise. Today, the slam of the door was the sound of cold loneliness.

He had pulled the door shut, but the icy wind had taken it out of his hands and slammed it with a dry, wounded sort of sound that put the final period at the end of a sad sentence. There were no sounds after that period.

He chafed his cold hands, trying to get the feeling and warmth back in. It was December 23rd, 1931, and Tom had never known a time like this in his life. He was only 41 years old, but he felt 90. Everyone felt 90 these days. He absently rubbed the aches from the back of his neck, feeling the grime of the construction dust. There was a time when he'd come home from his work feeling satisfaction at a job well done; the aches and fatigue were just marks of significance because he was good at what he did. Even when he hadn't been contracted, if he was in a job line-up for a new building being built, you could bet he'd be the first picked to work that day. He had a good eye, was accurate and could do multiple tasks, including the complicated dance of the riveters and throwers. They'd fire the rivets until they were red hot, take them by the tongs and throw them, sometimes 75 feet, to be caught and riveted in place right then and there. All this, mind you, while walking a catwalk of beams upwards of 80 stories off the ground. But his forte was masonry. No one had the touch and the speed of Thomas Murphy.

That had been a few years ago. Before the Crash. *Huh, crash*, he thought to himself. Perfect word. He felt wrecked, all right.

Tom slumped down into his favorite chair, the threadbare, green velvet one that felt like an old friend. God, he'd give anything to have a cold pint. Even that simple pleasure had been taken away from him by the temperance movement and their Eighteenth Amendment. Like his pint, it was always the simple things that were the hardest, perhaps because one became so used to them, they became the fabric of one's day. Not that they were taken for granted, but that they were the very foundation. But he missed the sound of Johnny's footsteps the most. Footsteps carried the promise of someone walking toward you. For conversation, for some laughs, for a quick hug when his son had a rough time from the local bully.

"Bah!" he said to no one, as he abruptly got up out of his chair, running his hand through his hair, trying to jostle the ache of the memories out of his mind. He went to the kitchen and started to fry up a bit of bacon in the cast iron pan, and then a little of the tomatoes from the canning his mother sent to him. He cut a thick slice of the day-old bread and sat down to enjoy his dinner. There was nothing better than soaking up bacon grease and the juice of tomatoes with a slice of bread. Simple.

As he was scrubbing up the dish and one pan that he'd dirtied, there was a knock at the door. A small smile crept up as he heard a loud booming voice, "Tommy boy! Open up! Don't make me sing Danny Boy to you again!"

"No! Not again!" he yelled back, amicably. He quickly went to the door of his basement flat, at the bottom of a respectable townhouse. "Jesus, Harry. I'd like to keep my apartment, if you don't mind."

At that Harry began a resounding,"Oooooooh Danny booooooooy!" Tom shoved him inside and slammed the door shut. Harry cackled in his good-natured, thunderous way. He always spoke several decibels louder than everyone else. He'd worked full time on the riveting crew for over twenty years now. They used to laugh at the younger guys who were starting to talk about wearing hearing protection. Sissy-boys. But, they kinda had a point.

"I brought you sumthin'," said Harry with a grin, showing his missing eyetooth. He brought out a lemonade bottle, but it had an amber liquid in it.

"Visiting the barbershop again, were you?" Tom asked while getting out two glasses. "Bless," he said, his Irish accent coming out in full-strength. "That, my friend, is a sight for sore eyes. Sláinte!" They clinked glasses in companionable silence, enjoying the smooth liquor "imported" from Canada and served at the local speakeasy behind the barbershop. Tom was too nervous about getting into any kind of trouble if the police were to raid the shop.

41

He wouldn't risk anything that might hinder his income or his ability to pay the rent for his home. His home was his last link to his memories, not to mention his security. If a man had a roof over his head to call his own, he had some dignity left.

As if reading his thoughts, Harry asked, "Have you heard anything from either of them?"

Shaking his head slowly, not looking up from his glass, "No. Nothing yet."

"Well," said Harry gruffly, "You only sent the letters a couple weeks ago, they probably–"

"Four weeks," Tom interrupted.

"Well, yeah, four weeks. Were you certain of the addresses?"

"As sure as I can be. It was the last address I heard of from John. He sent a postcard from Chicago. Mimi's I sent to her mother. But I don't even know the last time her mother heard from her."

Tom saw Harry's righteous indignation on his behalf written all over his face; he was such a loyal friend. He said, "You know better than that, Harry. They both had reasons. I'm no saint. Especially back then," he muttered.

Several years ago he'd been a different man. Hell, the world had been a different world. The Crash was hard in and of itself, but it was especially hard because it was such a bitter contrast to the life they'd been living. Like mistaking salt for sugar. The 20s made Tom feel invincible. Heady. Strong. Potent. Nothing could stop him. He'd worked hard, made money, invested some. He was working his way up to General Contractor. He was going to send John to the best school he could afford.

He should've seen signs. He should've paid more attention. It was like it was at the back of his mind but he'd treated it as if he had all the time the world. He might never have seen signs of the market collapse, but he should've seen the signs in his own wife. The small amounts of money missing from his billfold. Mimi making more trips to the hairdresser, grocer, friend's houses. His mother had always said he had a blind spot for redheads. Mimi could do no wrong, even though his mother had been perfectly honest with him that she had a hard time liking her. After Mimi left him, it took a few months, but he'd had an honest talk with his mother about her.

"Why didn't you like her, Mum?" he'd asked, earnestly wanting an answer. He thought he had it all figured out, but obviously he was in the dark.

"Well, honey, I felt like… Like she was crafty."

"Crafty?" he laughed uncertainly.

"Well, devious. I could never put my finger on it, but she was opportunistic. If she got invited to two parties, she'd figure out the best, most advantageous one to go to, even if it meant disappointing a good friend. Even with Johnny."

Tom recollected many times like that. He'd always figured she was just being efficient. But he started getting a glimpse into the motivation behind it. It was so opposite to how he handled life. He'd always talked with Johnny about standing up for his friends, about loyalty, and making noble choices.

"Even with Johnny? She'd do that with him, too?" he asked incredulously. He knew in his heart that she never really was the person he thought she was, to be able to not only walk out on her husband, but her son as well. But to hear about her being opportunistic with John, too? It was hard to wrap his mind around.

"Unfortunately, yes," said his mother. "Even John." She sipped her tea, watching him carefully. He knew in his heart that there was no one on the earth whom she cared for more, than her 41-year-old burly, intelligent but apparently naïve, son. She'd always been there for him. They had a special relationship that flowed into deep friendship. He thought back to the time when he'd fallen for Mimi. His mom had shared her own misadventures with him, trying to show him that love needed more than just attraction. But he just couldn't see anything but his love for Mimi. He was starting to learn now.

Tom had been lost in his own thoughts as his mother told him about Mimi's lack of character that day. Unfortunately, it made sense. He had needed to hear it. Then he'd suddenly barked out a loud laugh as he watched his slender, petite mother who was always decorous, take out a bottle of whiskey, pour a quick glass and slam it back as good as Harry would. She'd looked at him laughing at her and only said, "What? You want one, too?"

Tom could feel Harry's eyes on him as he'd been recollecting about Mimi and his mother. He'd been smiling

44

at this funny memory of his mum. "I'm just thinking of talking with my mother about it all."

Harry immediately smiled, chuckling, "Your mother. There's only one Caroline! I was just asking her today–"

Tom looked sharply at him, cutting off his words. "Today? You saw her today? Oh God. You didn't. You didn't run into her at the *barbershop*, did you?"

By this time, Harry was shaking he was laughing so hard. He finally let loose with the loud guffaw he'd been trying to hold back. "Ha! Ha! Ha! Of Course! That's exactly where I bumped into her, Tommy boy." It was absolutely infectious. Tom couldn't contain it either. They both laughed until they had to wipe tears from their eyes.

Later that night, Tom lay in his bed, listening to the sounds of the city. Tomorrow was Christmas Eve. Thank God he still had his mother. He was looking forward to time at her house, where he grew up. She had this indomitable spirit. And obviously, she was mischievous. He never had a friend who hadn't loved her. That alone should've given him pause concerning Mimi, he thought. She'd never come out to actually say she didn't like his mother; she probably knew that would've been a deal-breaker. He wasn't a mama's boy, but how could you not like Caroline?

Mimi had a habit of changing the topic if his mother came up in conversation. And most of his friends, now that he got to thinking about it, would end up at some point or other, sitting on a stool and chatting with his mum in the kitchen as she cooked dinner or cleaned up. It was something he and his sister had always done, too. But Mimi

45

never did that. Not once. His mother wasn't perfect by any stretch. She had a penchant for saying the wrong thing at the right time and the right thing at the wrong time. If she ever lined those things up, she'd be really amazing. Well, actually, part of her charm was that she fully embraced her weaknesses.

He knew he'd be able to get over Mimi. But John was another story. He missed his boy. John would be 20 this year. He hadn't seen him for two years. It felt like yesterday when he'd stomped out the door in a rage, the door slamming behind him. Tom should've gone after him. He had no idea John would stay away. He hadn't realized the boy had packed his bags; that he'd *planned* on leaving. And on staying gone. It wasn't until Tom walked back to his room to find it neat, almost empty in fact, and extremely lonely that he knew it. It was that moment that the finality of the slam of the door truly sank in. Tom still cringed with the thought of the last conversation they'd shared. He wished he could do it differently. He would. He would in a heartbeat.

"No, John," he'd said, "You will not. You will never go to school to be one of those bankers who just practically ruined our country! It's not a safe bet."

"Yeah, and you know all about that, don't you, Dad?" he said accusingly.

Tom flushed with equal parts shame and fury. "John Brennan Murphy."

"Dad, I'm sorry, but can't you understand that I know what's best for my own future? Maybe I can help America come back from all this. You know I'd be different from those businessmen who ruined everything. I just need the education to get to that point. Please listen!"

Tom shook his head slowly as he remembered his last, angry words to his son, "No! You will never do that and if you do I will never forgive you. I will always be disappointed in the man you've turned out to be."

Tom clenched his hands into fists as he relived those words once again. He still couldn't believe he'd said them. So hurtful. So cruel. No son should ever hear those words. God knows if his own mother said that to him, he'd crumble. And that's exactly how Johnny had looked. Tears came yet again, as Tom remembered – forced himself to remember every detail as penance – John's look of shock and utter despair, like his heart was being torn in two. Then it was followed up with a stubborn fury of his own. John picked up his bag and walked out the door.

Tom finally fell asleep although it was in the middle of the night that he at last succumbed. He woke up with a familiar pit in his stomach. All those words, all those mistakes. If only his new words, the words he'd learned in becoming the man he was today, could make it through to John. And Mimi. He was sure their marriage wasn't one to make a new start, but he at least wanted to make an end of it officially and for both of them to be able to move on.

The next morning, he drank his black coffee and got a roll at the corner vendor on his way to the construction site. He watched the people walking by on their way to work and school. He'd always lived in New York City. Couldn't imagine living anywhere else. Unlike most New Yorkers, he never took the city for granted. It was always new to him. He took pride in the fact that there were now seven buildings in this amazing skyline that he himself helped build with his own hands. Making history, forging a city. One that he was certain would carry on despite the Crash. Despite the Depression with its soup lines and broken lives. In fact, for a while, the clatter of the new buildings came to a stop on that infamous day in October two years ago. But it was the builders who figured out a way to carry on. This very day he was working on Rockefeller Center. Eight months ago, he'd helped finish the Empire State Building. Tallest building in the world. Now that was an accomplishment.

He'd even come up with some ideas that helped revolutionize building techniques. The Empire State Building was the first building with banks of elevators. Instead of all of them hitting every floor, some were designated for the higher floors only. That way the flow of people could keep moving. He'd thought about that idea when they were getting ready to bring in the bricks for the building, for which they'd usually shut down several blocks around the intended building, and by pure manpower haul those bricks in by wheelbarrow. He'd brought his idea to the contractor and suggested unloading the bricks into the cavernous basement of the building, and then letting the elevators carry up the loads from a more central point. It would also save the city from the shutdown of those busy streets. His idea was an instant success and was most probably the reason he'd gotten a promotion.

Rockefeller Center was a beacon of new design. And it stood for so much more. Originally it was going to have

John D. Rockefeller Jr.'s favorite architectural style: Gothic. Rockefeller had dearly wanted this, but he knew that they were at the doorway of a new era. And he wanted his buildings to have a design that signified the progress that they stood for. So he went against his own preference and chose the sleek art deco style. Rockefeller Plaza was the first in the world to house offices, shops, restaurants, broadcasting studios, and entertainment venues all in one place. A city within a city.

Now there's an interesting guy, thought Tom, not for the first time. The Rockefeller family lost half their fortune in the Crash. Enough to make you want to pack it all up and head to Tahiti. He was pretty sure that's exactly what he'd have done. But John D. Rockefeller Jr. went ahead with the plans for the city within a city, and even when the Metropolitan Opera withdrew as a partner, John funded the project and ran it himself, agreeing to be personally responsible for the loans. Boy what a party for the guys in construction that day! The project provided employment for 75,000 workers. But that was nothing compared to the sound of riveters and hammers and trucks rolling, hitting the air after the city seemed to have gone silent. It had died on that Black Tuesday. But then? It came back to life. People from all over the city came to watch the workers like him, and it was as if everyone was thinking, it's alive again! We can do it. Yeah, we can do it. Such a confident bastard, that Rockefeller.

And yet, why had Tom been so hard on Johnny when he'd wanted to do the same? It was like he just hadn't seen it that way. He'd been afraid, he admitted to himself. Afraid because his love of construction was all he really knew.

What if Johnny failed and he couldn't help him? He'd let that fear drive him, and it turned into anger and bitterness, like fear always does. And God help him, he'd been sorry every hour of his life since those final harsh words were said.

For the past few weeks, Tom had been feeling so antsy. As if there was something to be done, but he could never think of what it was. It ate at him. He thought once that it was because he almost forgot his mum's birthday (it was right after Thanksgiving), but that feeling didn't go away after the birthday. He mentally ticked down the list of things it could be. It wasn't a bill. It wasn't those letters he sent to Johnny and Mimi. With Mimi, he started to tell her he was sorry for how things turned out, but then that didn't seem quite right. He had tried his best with her, not that he was perfect. But he wasn't neglectful; he was affectionate, he provided for them well... So he ended up just reaching out to her and asking that they try to move on.

John, though. Well. That was a different letter. He knew exactly what he wanted to say. He loved him, and was deeply proud of him because of who he was. His choices in work and life were his to make. And he couldn't be more proud and thankful to have him as a son. And most earnestly, he said he was sorry. Couldn't be sorrier, in fact. They were hard words to write, you can be sure. He himself had never heard those words from his own father. But to not say them had become torture. Whether they were received or not, they had to be said. Even for his own sake.

"Well aren't we just a brooding mass of Irish stew?" said a familiar voice.

"Mornin' Mum, what are you doing around here?" he said, with a smile and an arm around her shoulders. She fairly brimmed with joy and her black coat was cheerily adorned with a cherry red scarf and a lapel pin in the shape of a Christmas tree.

"Oh, Tommy, you know I go all over the place. I was doing some errands and thought I might run into you. Don't forget, we have to trim the tree tonight! I invited some friends. You should invite Harry." Of course she did. Her house was never empty. She went on, in her effervescent way, "Just look at it here!" pointing out the red bows, a few scattered evergreen wreaths, and a man playing music on the corner. "Oh I just love those Christmas songs on the accordion! Lovely. You know, I heard Bing Crosby at a little club with Ethel last week. He wasn't supposed to be there on stage, but he just got up out of the crowd. And you know what he did? He started singing some Christmas hymns. Well, I can tell you, he puts a whole new spin on them!" Tommy had been struck speechless as he watched his mother speak fondly of the crooner, Bing, and even began to fan her face as she flushed with the memory of him singing. Good Lord.

"Mum. Mum. Please stop," he stuttered, half-horrified, half-laughing.

Consumed with thoughts of her night at the club, she suddenly looked up at him, as if surprised that he'd suddenly appeared. She chuckled her deep sort of laugh, "Tommy, you look even more handsome now that you're well and truly blushing." She wrapped her arm around his and they began to walk down the street together.

He had to admit, now that she'd brought his attention to something outside of himself, the city did have a nice feel to it. And the Christmas tree vendors added that delightful scent of the pine trees to many of the corners.

"You know, Tommy boy…" only she and Harry called him Tommy boy. It always made him feel good when they did. "I was reading an article yesterday about Christmas trees. Did you know, they began with the Vikings?"

"The Vikings? You're sure?" He cocked an eyebrow at her. She was a history buff, and was always sharing her interesting finds with him. But once in a while she confused her details. The Vikings sounded a little dubious.

Instead of being offended, she laughed, "I knew you'd say that. So I double-checked. They loved the evergreens. Being so far north, they had months of darkness and cold. They loved that the trees thrived even in the dead of winter. So they brought them indoors. They were symbols of life. And good fortune. Can you imagine? In months of total darkness, no sunshine, bitter cold, they considered themselves of good fortune. Beautiful, isn't it Tommy?"

"It is, Mum, it really is."

"There was also some silly story about that Martin Luther who supposedly saw the stars through the evergreens on a walk one night and he added candles to his Christmas tree as a sign of hope. But you know how I feel about him, Tommy. I'm not sure I can give him the credit this article did for the tree becoming a part of the Christmas celebration. I just can't do it, son. I can't!" Caroline was a devout Catholic. He himself didn't feel too troubled by

Martin Luther; he even agreed with some of his sentiments. But his mother had faced cruel bigotry as a young girl for being Catholic. She even had a brick lobbed at her once, and it hit her head, leaving a scar at her temple. He noticed she absently rubbed that spot as she spoke.

"It's alright, Mum," he said, as he gently rubbed her arm. "And what a great story! I'd always wondered how that got started. Remember the time Ruby got up into the tree and knocked it clear over?" He started reminiscing, trying to get her mind off Protestants.

She laughed, "Oh I'll never forget it, I won't. That cat! God love her, she was horrible about trees and curtains. A climber she was. Silly ginger cat."

They continued to share their memories of Christmases gone by. There were a lot of funny memories. Christmas was a hodge-podge of emotions for him. Probably for everyone. Funny and sad, with regrets and hopes for the future… Maybe that's what made it special, too. Not that it was wholly happy, but that it carried a wealth of emotion and reflection.

That antsy feeling was sharpening. There was definitely something Tom had to do. And he was getting closer to what it was. His time with his mother had heightened it. Well, whatever it was, for now, he had to get to work.

He spent most of the day creating a twelve-foot wall on the north side of the main structure, about 35 stories up. He'd gotten plenty used to the heights, and when he was concentrating on his work, he was completely absorbed, not minding one iota if he was a couple feet off the ground or several hundred. Lunchtime snuck up on him as it often did. He grabbed his lunch box and waved to Harry to join him up on a little ledge that gave them a fantastic view south, where the Empire State Building and the Chrysler buildings soared. That view never got old.

"Sugar and lard again, huh, Harry?" teased Tom.

"Oh yeah, Tommy boy. Mmmm!" he said, taking a big, happy bite of his first sandwich. Every single day, Harry's beloved lunch was a few sandwiches of white bread with a thick layer of lard sprinkled with sugar.

Tom wasn't exactly a fan. Not that lard and sugar was all bad, but he always appreciated his own sandwich of maybe an end of roast beef or a slice of ham, that much more.

"You coming over to mum's tonight?" asked Tom.

"Oh, wouldn't miss it. You know that," said Harry. Just as they were talking, a light snow began to fall. The sky had been looking like it might for the last couple of hours. It had that winter white look to it. They always felt the cold more at lunchtime. When they were working, it was actually nicer when it was colder out, as long as it didn't get down to the 20s. Then it was too cold and their fingertips would go numb.

"I was thinking," said Harry, "You know, I think we should invite a few more of the fellas over to your mom's place. I know she doesn't have that much room, but it would do them good." Tom knew what Harry meant. These had been hard years. Their friends had become more than just fellow workers in these tough times. Every single one of them felt hardship in some way. A few of them had lost kids in a bad scarlet fever season this past year. Tom's wasn't the only wife to walk out and there were new guys who he was pretty sure had walked out on their families. He could tell because they walked like they were carrying a heavy pack on their shoulders. Most of them could afford the necessities, thanks to these good jobs. But it was tight, there weren't many luxuries.

The fear was the hardest thing to set aside. They'd seen what could happen to the country, when prior to this, they'd felt invincible. America was where you went to be protected, to get a good life. Everyone felt that fear. Sometimes it was palpable, especially when you heard more news of bankers jumping out windows, businesses closing, families being torn apart. It was times like those that he and his buddies appreciated their jobs and their camaraderie the most. At least they could come together and work. They'd build something. Together. When you looked at what you all accomplished at the end of the day, that fear subsided a little.

In fact, the guys had gotten into a habit of standing together just for a minute at the end of their shift. They could see the progress and appreciate it.

"I got it!" he shouted, scaring Harry and almost making him drop his hot coffee.

"What? You okay boy-o?" Harry asked, wiping some coffee off the front of his coat.

"Ha ha ha!" Tommy laughed, with his barrel-chested guffaw. "I got it. I've been thinking about something for days and I finally got it."

"What'd you get?" Harry asked dubiously.

"You'll see."

Shortly they got back to work. Tom was lost in his own thoughts so Harry left him to it.

Tom always worked hard, but today he was like a machine. Bricks slipped almost effortlessly into place. The mortar was the perfect consistency and he didn't have to tinker much to get it that way. The wall went up fast and about 20 minutes before the end of their shift he went over to Harry.

"Harry!" he shouted over the din. It was enough to get Harry to look over at him. Tom made some complicated hand signals that meant he'd be right back, cover for him. Harry nodded. Tom fairly ran off, feeling a sense of excitement he hadn't felt in a long time.

Tom ran all four blocks, found exactly what he was looking for and started back to the work site carrying his heavy and awkward parcel. Just as he was about to get to the entrance to the site where the public was cordoned off, he saw a tall man with a black suit taking a good look at the building, both hands on his hips blocking the way into the site.

"Excuse me, sir, could you move over please? I need to get through with this," said Tom. The man slowly put his hands down to his side and turned around.

Tom dropped his heavy burden right to the ground in shock. The man before him was Johnny. Johnny looked exactly like Tom felt, completely stunned, his eyes wide open from surprise. Then Johnny collected himself and looked like he was preparing for a well-rehearsed speech. In fact, he pulled out a note in his pocket like he was about to consult his notes.

"John," said Tom. His voice made John slowly bring his eyes up to look into his father's eyes. Before John could even take a good look at him, Tom took one huge stride and suddenly he was squeezing John in a bear hug that brought his feet off the ground, despite his six-foot-one stature.

"Dad, I'm sorry, too." Which made Tom squeeze him harder. "Dad. Can't breathe," said John, trying unsuccessfully not to grin.

Tom set him down, but didn't take his hands off the shoulders of his son. He looked him square in the eyes. Those same blue eyes of his mother. "John. Those words I said to you… I'm so sorry. They are unforgivable. I'll always be so proud of you, son."

"Dad. You're wrong."

Tom's smile faded with concern. "What do you mean?" he asked.

"Your words are completely forgiven." Tom's smile came back.

"What made you come back?" asked Tom.

"Your letter. And, well. Mamo," said Johnny rather sheepishly.

"Ha ha!" laughed Tom. "Mamo? Your grandmother? Of course. Of course," he snickered.

John couldn't help himself and started laughing as well. "Da! You wouldn't believe it. But about a week after I received your letter, the doorbell rang at my apartment. Mamo stood on my front porch in her little red skirt suit, all five feet of her, and bawled me out. She was as loud as Harry!"

By now, Tom was wiping tears from his eyes from the thought of his own little mum finding John, going to him, and giving him a thorough scolding. "Oh Johnny, she shouldn't have done that. It was my fault."

"Well, Da, she said as much, but she knew I was just as hard-headed as you. And she knew about your letter. So when I hadn't made a move to make things right, she felt she had to step in." John looked off into the distance, "Damn, she was scary."

"Ha ha ha!" laughed Tom all over again. "Oh don't I know it? Welcome to the club, my boy." They both took a couple of deep breaths, fully appreciating the peace that neither of them had truly known in over two years.

"It's good to be back, Da. The building looks great! Hey, looks like you have some plans. Maybe I could give you a hand?" asked John, nodding with a smile at the package Tom had dropped at their feet.

"Oh, that's the best idea I've heard in a long time," said Tom. "Come on."

They walked together into the work site. Over in the center, was the bunch of fellows John had come to know as well as a group of uncles, so Tom could barely stand the surprise that was about to take place. Their backs were turned to them, their hands on their hips, taking a good look at the job of the day.

"Do I have a surprise for you boys!" yelled Tom, making all of them turn around at once.

"Johnny!" yelled Harry, the first to realize who the tall guy was next to Tom. Harry was a large man. But boy he could run. All 250 pounds of him came running, vaulting over any bricks or pipes lying in his way. Tom saw Johnny brace himself. Harry was like built like a locomotive and he barreled right into both of them, almost tackling them to the ground.

The others came over and there was a lot of backslapping, hand-shaking and general merriment. Harry said loudly to Tom, "Do you have a plan here, Tommy Boy?" nodding at the long package on the ground in the middle of the group of guys.

"Now that is a damn good idea!" said a familiar voice behind the group.

They all turned around together. "Ma!" they all cheered. Most of them considered Caroline a second mother. But it was Tom who caught her up and swung her around.

"Thank you, Mum," he gruffly whispered into her ear as he set her down gently.

"I love you, my boy," she said. "Now! Let's get to work!"

Everyone ran in different directions. Tom and John picked up the package and walked to a raised platform in the center of all the activity, and in full sight of all the people walking by on the surrounding sidewalks and streets. The carpenters made a quick and sturdy stand. Then John and Tom eased the large trunk into it. Caroline cut the bottom cords and they all unwrapped the burlap from a tall blue spruce, its spicy branches unfolding and opening up as if it was greeting them all.

The carpenters, always quick with their hands, brought over long paper chains. The demolition guys brought blasting caps. Everyone brought something to decorate the tree in their own way. When it felt like it was complete, they all stood around; their faces still dirty from their day's work, debris from the site all over the ground, and their 20-foot tree a homely but stunningly beautiful sight. Silence overtook them all. That day, they stood not only before the day's work, but the work of something else. They all got the feeling that something important was happening. Something that would carry this day forward and be remarkable. It was a kind of Holy ground.

Caroline held Tom's hand on one side, and Johnny's hand on the other. Harry, feeling the preciousness of the moment, softly then more fully, in his deep baritone began singing, "The first Noel… the angels did say… was to certain poor shepherds in fields as they lay…" Everyone joined in, the music lifting over their heads, over their tree and carrying out to the buildings, the people, and the city they loved.

Outside their circle, stood a man with his hands clasped behind his back. A small smile crept across his mouth, knowing the importance of this moment. He slowly nodded and said almost to himself, "Now that is a good idea indeed." After enjoying a few more songs, he slowly turned and thoughtfully walked away.

"Evenin' Mr. Rockefeller! Merry Christmas!" shouted a young boy as he passed by waving cheerily.

"Merry Christmas, son. Merry Christmas."

CHAPTER 6

I had stopped typing a long time ago. But the story held such clarity in my mind, I knew I'd be able to replicate it easily. We paused for a few thoughtful moments, both Billy and I thinking about the Murphy family and that incredible moment of the first tree going up. "Now *that* is an incredible story," I said.

Billy's eyes sparkled with the happiness of having shared something with someone who thought it was just as cool as he did. "But how do you know about this story? You know one of the family members, don't you?" I asked.

His grin grew wider. "Let's see if you can figure it out. I'm 82. I was born in 1933."

"A friend of the family?" I guessed. He shook his head. Yeah, that wasn't right, Billy knew intimate details. Let's see. It was 1931 when Tom and John were reconciled. Could he be John's son? I asked, "John's son?"

He shook his head, "You're getting closer. It's even better." I swear if he wasn't so dignified, he'd have giggled. He was having a marvelous time.

"No! You mean… Is Tom your *father*?"

He fairly shook with happiness as he nodded. "Yes. About a year after the Christmas tree, my father married again. He was in his forties, and my mother, Sarah, was a widow and in her early thirties. They met and instantly fell in love. I came along a year later."

"Oh my. So Caroline is your grandmother, Johnny is your half-brother," I said, putting it all together. He nodded again. "What happened with the rest of them?"

"Johnny did go into business and was quite successful. He married and had four children. I was close with his children since our ages were similar. He was like an uncle to me and we always shared a special connection. Grandma Caroline remained mischievous and was like a second mother to Sarah. They laughed together more than schoolgirls. It was at those moments my father was the happiest. We never did hear of Mimi again. John was saddened by that, but it's just the way it is. The marriage between her and Tom was dissolved; a judge declared abandonment."

"What about the Rockefellers? Did they start doing the tree tradition right away?"

"No, it wasn't until 1933 that the tradition actually started. But John Jr. was a religious man. That Christmas Eve where he witnessed the tree that the construction workers set up had a powerful effect on him. After I got a few degrees in history, the Rockefeller family approached me about working as a Rockefeller historian. I personally think they knew of the story about my family having a link with the construction and the tree, too."

We wrapped up our time and I thanked him profusely. I promised to keep him updated about my articles coming out. Then he had one last suggestion, "You know, Jane, since you're doing the history of Christmas traditions, I have a friend you should speak with about the song *O Holy Night*. There's a story you should hear." He gave me the name of a woman who lived down in the West Village. "I'll make a call. She'll be delighted. Could you meet tomorrow?"

"Absolutely!" Boy, was he efficient.

I left the office, continuing to make mental notes and adding a few questions and thoughts to the notes in my phone. Just then I received a text, "Drew here. Where r u?"

Ooh, we're texting now. "Near St. Pats," I responded.

"Feeling pious are we?"

"Funny."

"I want to hear about your day. Would you like to meet for dinner?"

"Yes." Yes I did. "Great day! Tomorrow learning about O Holy Night."

"Great! Can't wait to talk. Let's say 7 at Felice on First Ave at 83rd."

"C U then!"

Well, that would be fun. I started thinking through questions I had for him, too. I had to figure out how to ask about Willow. Maybe I could just share the letter with him. I felt possessive about that letter. I liked it. And I liked Willow and the man who wrote it. So there was part of me that wanted to keep it to myself.

I walked into St. Patrick's Cathedral and beheld the majesty of that cavernous, gorgeous place. There were a lot of people, but everyone was respectful. The huge, circular stained glass window up at the altar was incredible. The ceiling soared to the heavens and I remembered the history of the groundbreaking architecture of flying buttresses that allowed for these high ceilings without needing columns to hold them up. It's funny how one idea could change the face of the whole world. Why that one lesson about ancient historical architecture stood out to me so much, I wasn't sure. But the thought of the buildings, up to that point, being so low, so strapped down to the earth, and to think all of a sudden you could see buildings that reached to the sky out of all the flat villages… it had to have been unbelievable to witness.

I took my time as I enjoyed looking around and pondering some of the things I heard from Billy. I would've loved to meet Caroline. She was so different from my mother.

After walking back to my hotel and changing, I found my way up to Felice. The Italian restaurant sparkled with wine glasses and single taper candles on each small table, mixed with dark woods and great textures. I found Drew already at a table in the far corner. I'd changed into a black dress and heels, feeling more formal since we were going out to dinner. I thought I looked pretty good, as the neckline was a wide boat neck. My blond curls just reached my shoulders and I always thought dark colors looked great against my hair.

I took a look at Drew, and the way he was looking at me, I figured he thought the same thing. He was wearing a black suit with dark blue shirt. He looked pretty fine himself. We were grinning at each other before we could say a word and said at the same time, "You look great!" Which broke any ice in sight.

We ordered a bottle of wine and I started right in with the incredible story I'd heard from Billy that day. Drew listened intently and we were half-way through the bottle of wine before I finished.

"That is a fantastic story, Coco!"

I laughed, "You're really going with Coco, huh?"

"I think it's quite fitting," he said with a smirk. "Besides, it goes with your wonderful eyes." His smirk softened to a gentle smile.

"My eyes?" Whoa.

"Yeah, they're a beautiful brown with little gold flecks..." He paused for a long, tense moment looking into my eyes. All right, maybe the color brown isn't so bad after all.

He coughed. "Uh. Oh, hey! There's an assistant from work," he said in a saved-by-the-bell voice. "I asked him to bring me something you'll like." He waved over a young man who had just entered the restaurant.

He bounded over to our table and said, "Here you go Mr. Davis!"

As he handed the packet of papers to Drew I asked, "Don't you mean Clompsburg?"

Drew looked up at me and the boy said, "What's a clompsburg?"

"Oh brother," I said as Drew snorted and I took a sip of wine. The boy left, giving me a look as if he was unsure if he should leave his boss in the hands of such a weirdo. "Clompsburg, huh? I should've realized."

"Well... You have a thing about names. I thought I'd have a little fun with you."

"I like it," I said. "My brother did the same sort of thing to his girlfriend. They'd been friends, but when he asked her out, they were going to meet up with my dad for a beer first. He'd told her that dad had been a weatherman all his life. She'd thought that extremely interesting, so when my dad finally came to the bar and sat down, she said, 'So Jim tells me you're a meteorologist!' Without as much as a blink of an eye, my dad said, 'Yes I am!' He's a tax attorney."

Drew was laughing. It was one of the only times where my dad displayed some fun wit beneath his not-so-shiny exterior. "They told her, of course, and she has a great sense of humor, so it was all good."

We ordered dinner. I was interested in those papers. "What did your assistant who's concerned for my sanity bring you?"

"Well. Since you said you're getting a story on *O Holy Night,* I did some research on it for you and found some interesting things. I'm getting a new printer at home tomorrow, so I asked the office to print out some things for you to read."

"I'll look through the papers later. What did you find out? Tell me about it."

"First, a priest, a Jew and a poet walk into a bar."

"Pardon?" I asked.

"Right?" he said. "Sounds like a joke. But it's how the song got started."

"Seriously?"

Drew nodded and started telling me the long tale of the hymn that I hated to admit that I loved. The way he dove into the history, I knew I had a history major or maybe a poli-sci guy on my hands.

O Holy Night had a twisting story starting with a wine merchant in France in 1847. Basically, Placide Cappeau de Roquemaure was a poet and although he never stepped into a church, a priest in his small village asked him to write a poem for the Christmas service. Placide decided to use the Gospel of Luke as his guide and started to imagine the birth of Jesus in Bethlehem as a starting point and wrote Cantique de Noel. Placide loved his new poem and knew he wanted a quality musician to back it up. So he asked his friend Adolphe Charles Adams, a famous composer, to write the music.

By this time our meal had arrived and I was enjoying a fantastic mushroom ravioli. Drew carried on, "The other quality that made Adolphe an obvious choice to write the music for this Christmas poem was his Jewish friend."

"Wait, what?" I asked.

He chuckled. "I know. But, despite these words representing a holiday he didn't celebrate or believe in, he was moved by the lyrics. Surprisingly quickly, their song became part of Catholic Christmas masses all over.

"But then, wait till you hear this… Placide ended up becoming a part of the socialist movement. That, mixed with the fact that the church leaders later discovered that Adolphe was a Jew, meant the song ended up being completely denounced by the church even though Cantique de Noel had been widely loved throughout France."

"How is that possible?" I asked.

"Yeah. How did they say it? Let me see…" Drew shuffled through the papers until he found the right one. "Here it is, they deemed it as unfit for church services because of its lack of musical taste and total absence of the spirit of religion."

"What!"

"Stop yelling, Coco." I snorted.

"But it didn't stop the French people from loving the song and still singing it."

"Good."

"Mm," he murmured as he nodded, enjoying his pollo milanaise. "A decade later, enter in the American John Sullivan Dwight."

"There's *more*?"

He nodded, thoroughly enjoying himself. He told me most of the story as if he'd memorized it, only checking his notes to read the exact lines he needed. "Dwight was a graduate of the Harvard College and Divinity School. He became a Unitarian minister, but dealt with anxiety attacks every time he had to speak in front of the congregation and couldn't continue in the ministry. He was a wonderful writer and founded Dwight's Journal of Music. For 30 years, he was the editor when one day he discovered Cantique de Noel and wanted to introduce it to America.

"Besides loving the song for its poetry and incredible

music, he was an abolitionist and was moved by the lines, *Truly he taught us to love one another; his law is love and his gospel is peace. Chains shall he break, for the slave is our brother; and in his name all oppression shall cease!* Dwight translated it into English and published it in his magazine and several other songbooks. *O Holy Night* became popular in America fast, especially in the North during the Civil War."

"Talk about a twisting tale!" I said, sipping my wine and considering ordering a cappuccino. I'm not a big dessert fan. Unless I can drink it. Or if it's a cookie.

"It's good stuff," said Drew. After a few minutes of finishing our meal in companionable silence, we ordered coffee for Drew and a cappuccino for me.

"So… history or poli-sci?" I asked with an eyebrow cocked.

"Awww, you saw right through me. Poli-sci."

"What do you do now?" I asked.

"I'm a lawyer."

Usually you get a litany of what kind of law a lawyer practices, but Drew was quiet on the matter. "Why are you quiet? Don't you want to tell me what kind of law you practice?" I asked in my usual delicate way.

"I handle social justice issues. I've worked with IJM in the past."

"International Justice Mission? Nice. I've done a couple of articles on their efforts."

"Yeah, thanks. Then I found I have a penchant for helping families fight for what was stolen in past wars." His dark eyes suddenly took on a knowing intensity, looking right into mine.

"Oooh. You're ready to talk about Willow," I said.

He made a sort of strangled sound. I think he thought it would take me longer to read his mind. It didn't. "Uh, yes. I guess I am. How do you know about her?"

I sat back in the cushioned seat, cupping my cappuccino in both hands. I looked at him intently for a few minutes, deciding how to approach this delicate subject. He was ready to talk, but guarded. Whatever happened in the past with Willow, it had a strong effect on him. He took pains to relax his shoulders and smooth out the look of concern on his face. But his hands gave him away and I feared for the life of the coffee cup in his hand.

"Drew," I said with a little laugh. "Don't punish the coffee cup." I carefully reached out and touched his hand that had been gripping the cup handle with malice aforethought. A crackle of electricity hit my fingertips as I touched him. It's funny how that happens. It's rare. I gently pressed his hand to the table, freeing the poor cup.

He must've felt the tingle of electricity, too. His dark eyes became darker as he smiled.

"Well, quite honestly, I don't know how it came into my possession, but I have a partial letter written to her," I said.

His cup almost clattered to the floor. "What? Oh my god. She has the letter. Oh my god." He'd said this almost to himself, and that static hit the air that happens when something of huge importance just took place, like witnessing a car accident. His face was white, but deep down I saw something like hope flicker. "Could I please *see* it?"

"Yes! Of course! But you have to tell me more. You have to tell me the whole story." He was barely looking at me any longer. He was distracted and you could practically see the gears in his mind turning at break-neck speed. "Drew.

Drew!"

"What? Oh, yes. Do you have the letter on you?"

"No, it's back at the hotel."

"She doesn't have the letter. That's okay, because I need to get a few things in order. Oh my god."

"Drew. Dude. You're acting very strangely. Want to enlighten me a little? *Where are you going?*"

In a split second, he was standing and pulling on his suit coat. He looked at me then and, although his thoughts were unreadable, his face showed two things intermingling: hope and fear.

"Coco. I'm so sorry. I know this is weird. Just keep that letter safe. I'll... I'll see you tomorrow. I have to check on something. Can you...? Can you just trust me and wait for the information? I promise I'll tell you everything."

Well, since he put it that way. And there was no denying the earnest expression on that handsome face. "Absolutely. Of course. I want to help." The hopeful part of his expression took over the fearful part. Suddenly he smiled bigger than I'd seen yet and before I knew it, he'd reached behind my head and bent in to give me one of the best kisses of my life.

"Holy–" I stuttered, as he broke away and then practically ran out the door.

The waiter came over at that fortuitous moment and I expected to get the check, since Cinderella apparently had to leave suddenly. But he was grinning cheekily and said, "Don't worry. Mr. Davis has a tab here. He's a regular. He'd kill me if I gave you the bill."

"So. Does he run off like that a lot?" I asked, taking another sip of my cappuccino.

"No!" he laughed out. "In fact! He's usually so serious.

I'm always trying to get him to crack the smile. I've never seen him more smiling and the chuckling before." His Italian accent was charming. His intelligent eyes shone as he summed up the night pretty well, "I think something interesting and very importante is happening tonight. Ciao, bellisima."

❧

The following day, I hadn't heard from Drew before I made my way down in a cab to the West Village. Billy had called to say he'd set up an appointment at the Bosie Tea Parlor at 10 o'clock in the morning for tea.

I got out and decided to walk around and enjoy the drastic difference of this area from mid-town, where my hotel was located, and from the Upper East Side where Drew lived. Everything was shorter, only reaching maybe six stories at the most. The buildings were much older and very quaint. Red brick townhouses, little boutiques, and unique bars lined the streets. Getting around was confusing; there was no grid here and the street maps looked like a bowl of spaghetti. Thank God for Google Maps. Again. I stopped at Sheridan Square to sit on a bench for a few minutes. So far I was enjoying my adventure to New York City quite a bit. The people watching was sensational. Feeling rested, I walked over to the Bosie Tea Parlor.

I was early, but my appointment was earlier. I walked into the quaint little café and I saw my appointment. Because she was waving frantically, as if I couldn't see her in the little café stuffed with books and small tables holding yummy looking treats. It was like she was hailing a cab. If the waving hadn't made a scene, her voice certainly did.

"JANE!!! I'M HERE, JANE SMITH!!!" Three customers had been startled into spilling their tea, two more had been quietly talking and were trying to figure out just what the falderal was about, and half a dozen or so were looking like they were glad they weren't in my shoes.

I said to the roomful, "I can't be sure, but I think that's my appointment."

I walked over to meet my date. I said, "Hello, I'm Jane Smith. Nice to meet you Mrs. Foxmorten." I admit a part of me wondered if Drew had gotten his hands on the name of this woman. I don't *think* he'd do that… Maybe.

Luckily for me, she toned down her exuberance at least a couple of decibels. I still noticed a few people subtly scooching their chairs farther away. I mouthed to one of them behind me, "Good idea."

"Well, Ms. Smith, I am so delighted that Billy called me! I couldn't be happier to meet you and to tell you this story! It hasn't been told and I said to my grandchildren, I said, someone needs to tell Poppy's tale!" I started smiling in earnest. She was so genuine, so all-out-there, I just liked her. At that moment, though, I was concerned about how I would ever author this part of the story because I was pretty certain proper grammatical structure wouldn't allow for the excessive use of exclamation marks, capital lettering, and bold face that would be truly necessary to convey Mrs. Foxmorten's actual exuberance.

Apparently, Billy and Mrs. Foxmorten had been friends for years and he of course had heard her story. I listened as she told me about their friendship and her life here in New

York City. The table was laden with a champagne tea service. I sipped the bubbly and eyed the scones with clotted cream, several kinds of tea sandwiches and macarons. I asked her if I could record her story, figuring a recording would be much easier to convert to text at another, more peaceful place and time.

It turns out, *O Holy Night* has another special place in history. As the tale unfolded, I found myself wishing I could be at another incredible moment in time. Oh, to be in that dark place, full of loneliness, and then hearing for the first time in recorded history, music appearing out of nowhere.

CHAPTER 7

Brant Rock, Massachusetts
December 1906

"Do you really have to go?" asked Poppy. It was only a few days before Christmas and he knew that this assignment would mean he wouldn't be home for Christmas. It was just part of life in the Navy. His wife, Cassandra, understood, but he was sure his ten-year-old daughter, Poppy, did not. Well? It couldn't be helped. And he wasn't all that crazy about the hubbub of Christmas anyway. It was a lot of bother. In the Navy, everything was simple, clean, even austere. You worked better that way. It was more efficient.

Christmas was messy, thought Peter. Sure, he'd miss his family, but he could skip the mess that meant awkward family get-togethers with the difficult family members (the rest of the year you could avoid them). He could skip all those messy decorations (the pine needles got into everything!). He would miss the food, though. Even though it meant a messy kitchen, that food was *good.* On top of all that, things at home were complicated, too. Cassandra was pregnant again and she was harder to live with. He loved her dearly, but when she was pregnant her mood was hard to figure out. She didn't talk to him like she did when she wasn't pregnant. He couldn't figure her out. See? Messy.

He always worried about her when he was gone, especially when she was pregnant, but several days away wasn't that terrible. And his mother-in-law would be around to help out so Cassandra wouldn't be on her own. Yeah, maybe it was better this way.

❧

Poppy was mad. Not sad – mad. She just couldn't understand her father. They had a pretty good relationship, but boy, at Christmas (her favorite time of year!) he was just extra difficult. It was like he wasn't really there even when he was standing right in front of her. And he was always reprimanding her for something. She just couldn't see what he saw. She'd see the glittery masterpiece she just made, while he'd see that she spilled glue on her shoe. Poppy would be consumed with the beautiful illustrations in her book and he'd tell her she had crumbs in her hair from the toast she'd been eating. She'd literally had no idea that the crumbs were there. Besides, who cares about the stupid toast? She'd have to work on him. She'd shake him awake if she had to!

Her teacher always said she was a firecracker. She certainly felt like one today! Honestly, it is what it is if you're in the Navy and you're called out and will be gone Christmas Eve. But to look relieved! That was unacceptable. Her dad had no idea what he was missing out on. The food! The family! The colorful decorations! Not to mention the fruit cake that only their family made. It took six weeks to marinate the fruit. It wasn't that dried up, weird, green and red fruit in the fruitcakes that weighed about ten pounds. Theirs had vanilla pudding in it, you made it in a special circular pan that looked like a wreath, and the marinated fruit was delicious.

The number one thing her dad was always telling her was, "Clean up your mess!" All the time. Every day. It was wearing on her. She was a good girl. Well, most of the time. There was the time when she locked all the teacher's bathroom stalls shut by crawling underneath the stalls. Boy did they have problems! She hadn't been caught, but she was pretty darn sure Mrs. Allen knew it had been her. Mrs. Allen was a big woman. Who used the bathrooms a lot. Poppy tried her hardest to not look guilty when Mrs. Allen berated the class about the prankster who had tampered with the bathroom. The best way to do that was not to try, but to focus on something else. So she recited some of her favorite stories in her head, focusing on the exact words. It was what saved her. Because it was *so funny!* She also hadn't made the mistake (this time) of telling her friend Wendall about it. He couldn't bear to be in trouble and if he knew she'd done it, he'd give it away by turning bright red and trying too hard not to look at Poppy, effectively pointing right at her.

She thought that maybe she was extra annoyed with her father, because it had been such an incredible year. And Christmas was a special time to think about the year that just finished. It was one year that would never be forgotten in her family's life nor in the country, perhaps. She wondered if people would hear the year 1906 and always associate it with one thing of horrific proportions. The San Francisco earthquake and fire. Of course, it was more real to her and even more terrifying because her own father had been there. He'd been serving directly under Lieutenant Frederick Freeman on a ship called the *Perry*. It was technically called a U.S.T.B.D. A United States Torpedo Boat Destroyer.

Her father never told them much about his work with the Navy. But around April 30th, he'd finally come home to Massachusetts on the train across the entire country, and in a few long hours he shared more about his work and his Navy life than she or her mother had ever heard in their life. Peter wasn't one to verbally share his feelings. Ever. He was a secret, sealed-up sort of man. Like a trunk that has a big, iron lock on it and you're always wondering what's inside. But she and her mother stayed stock-still as he unloaded his burdens, unwilling to let a sound or a movement stop him from revealing his thoughts and cares.

It was rare for men to share these things with women, despite the fact that they were smack in the middle of the Progressive Age. She thought he'd been in shock or something. And he never talked about it ever again. But she'd never forget it; she wouldn't want to. She had this desire to grasp onto life. Soak it up. So she wouldn't want to forget the horrible things in history – it was part of the fabric of life itself. Most of all, she didn't want to forget those hours of honesty from her dad. He'd never been so... revealed before. So open.

❧

Peter told his family almost everything about battling the fires after the earthquake. He couldn't believe later on that he'd shared so much. He couldn't help himself. It was like it all just poured out of him. There wasn't a day that went by that he didn't think about that time.

He and his crew had been aboard ship in the Pacific. After the earthquake, they left Mare Island with Freeman being in temporary command of a destroyer ship convoying all available nurses and surgeons from the Yard to the city of San Francisco. A Yard fire tug and a fireboat preceded them to the city. They'd let the surgical crew out then headed down to the Howard Street dock. They found the battalion chief of the fire department and they all jumped in to the fray, trying to save the city. The crews of the three ships worked without rest until the fire was under control four days later. Peter had never been so tired. The poor San Fran guys had to leave the waterfront posts if they got word their own homes were in danger. The men fought and fought, keeping to their posts until they collapsed.

It was a time where he saw the best and worst of humanity. His own crew thought nothing of giving all of themselves to this task. The city looked like a child's game of wooden blocks that had been smashed and toppled. Then set on fire. The helpless people, the children, the elderly, the hospital patients... It ripped their hearts apart.

But what he could never get over was the worst parts of humanity. Especially all along the waterfront, crowds of men and women rushed into the saloons and looted the stocks of liquor, becoming stupefied by the alcohol and too tired to even move out of the way of the fire itself.

That whole day they'd needed able bodies to rescue women and children in the poor residence district of Rincon Hill. The fire had made a clean sweep of the whole area in about an hour's time. But Peter and his handful of men couldn't do what they desperately needed to do. It was too much. And perfectly able-bodied men refused to help the fire department, saying they wouldn't work for less than 40 cents an hour. More than double the average wage! Men refused to aid even old and crippled men and women out of the way of the fire. He'd never seen such callous selfishness.

All the while the Navy men, who called different cities their home, fought as if this was their own. The harsh juxtaposition of this selfishness against utter selfless sacrifice was hard to comprehend. He and his friends had much of their facial hair burnt off. Their lungs hacked up black, disgusting gunk. Their muscles shook from fatigue; he could barely feel his fingers from gripping fire hoses, axes, and rifles so hard and so long. He even saw his buddy, Brownie, fall to the street and gash his head on a broken pipe. Only to get up, wrap a bandage around his head, and keep on moving without looking back. Just as Brownie was tucking in the ends of his bandage, he saw a little girl with two bare feet almost black from burns start to collapse. Brownie managed to catch her before she hit the ground and carried her to a hospital crew.

Peter and his men had gotten rifles and ammunition to help patrol at times, too. The quake had hit on April 18th. About five days later, they saw ferry boats coming in from Oakland. The water sources along the front were exhausted and the suffering was intense. The ferries, unbelievably, did not contain water or help of any kind. They contained thousands of sightseers. The ghoulish capacity of human beings would haunt him forever. They swarmed in, scattering about the city to witness this intense time of loss. And they joined in the looting.

At the same time, he saw the opposite. German and British ships came to the harbor to help. In particular, he remembered a Captain Sanderson of the ship *Martfield* who gallantly came to the rescue. He saved lives and property, even using his own ship as a refuge for the women and aged. He and his men even helped fight the fire.

After securing the waterfront, they headed up to Telegraph Hill, Broadway, Montgomery and Jackson streets. There was a completely different spirit in the city over there. The citizens offered every aid to the fire fighters. Peter's men showed the greatest daring and perseverance; their best work was accomplished there. They'd climb to the tops of buildings and extinguish fires from windows and cornices. They'd go through large buildings to tear down inflammable things like curtains and awnings in an attempt to thwart more fuel being added to the fires. This area was saved due to their efforts.

But just on the other side of Telegraph Hill, the fire was consuming one city block every half hour. One crew tried dynamiting four houses in an attempt to destroy the fuel for the fire and stop it. It didn't work. At one point a sulfur works was burning and the wind was blowing a gale. Showers of cinders, some three and four inches square, made this spot a purgatory. Even so, they kept on and the fires were eventually stopped.

Peter found soot in his hankies for months. He'd have scars on his hands and face for the rest of his life. But the main problem for him was wrapping his mind around the chaos. How did one human commit selfish atrocities, then another human from the same background, the same city, the same everything... commit noble sacrifice after noble sacrifice that saved other fellow men? How was that possible? It was the ultimate mess.

He still had nightmares about it all. And they got worse as Christmas time neared. Shouldn't it get better as the dates approached this family holiday? But he'd always been uncomfortable with Christmas. There was an incident at a house up at the top of Telegraph Hill that he'd think about forever, unsure of what it all meant. There were burnt ruins everywhere. But at this place, there was a box of Christmas ornaments. He'd brought them out of the still smoking home that had been all but destroyed. It brought him to tears as he saw the remnants of red bows, candle holders for the Christmas tree, and even the Christmas angel for the top of the tree, all singed black.

An elderly lady suddenly appeared next to him. She'd spied the box, too. She crept up slowly to the box, having recognized it. This black crater had once been her home. He watched with horrid fascination as she inched toward the box. But she wasn't crying. Her small hand reached in and pulled out a card and one little silver frame from the middle of the box, untouched from the smoke and fire. Her smile was... beautiful. She looked at him then.

"You saved this, didn't you?" she asked, her smile reaching her eyes and making her seem at least 20 years younger.

"I'm sorry I couldn't save more..." Peter said.

She cut him off with a hand on his arm. "Oh, don't be foolish. I saw you working. I've seen you save people. My neighbors. My family." She looked intently at his face that had to have been gray or black and he must have smelled just awful. It felt like she could see into his soul. But it didn't make him feel uncomfortable. He let her keep looking. "You saved more than you know. Thank you." And she left.

Why did that box mean so much to her? Why was that encounter a part of those nightmares and dreams? Something about it made him uncomfortable with Christmas. And relieved that he'd be out to sea for it.

ॐ

It was December 23rd and Poppy had an errand to do. She was walking across the street to her favorite neighbor's house. Mr. Fessenden. She even held one of their famous fruit cakes in her hands to give him as a present. She liked him. His first name was Reginald. When no one else was around, she called him Reggie. It was far too casual and disrespectful to call an elder by his first name, but he was a family friend and he liked her sense of humor. If she said something out of line around a lot of adults, she'd quickly look at him and he'd wink at her. That made her feel much better.

His house was a tangle of wires, weird machines, tools, and even a huge tower coming right up out of the top of his house. She would've loved to live in a mysterious home like that! Mr. Fessenden was a radio expert. He was like a magician. He could communicate with people all over the place through Morse code and he worked the telegraph like lightning. She never got tired of watching him work. He even taught her how to work the machine and she sent messages to his niece Florence in Detroit, Michigan. It was better than a pen pal! It was like they were secret spies.

She got to his house and since the whole spy idea really took root in her mind, she'd developed a secret knock to let him know it was her. Three quick knocks, three quick knocks, three quick knocks, two quick knocks. Or you could sing Jingle Bells to the beat (jingle bells, jingle bells, jingle-all, the way). She heard his voice through the door, "Come on in Popover!"

She carefully opened the door and walked in. His wife was a sweet, quiet woman and she knitted all the time. Poppy hated knitting. She tried not to dislike the woman just because she was a knitter. But the wife wasn't there today and she saw Mr. Fessenden in the back room, his workroom.

"I have a present for you!" she exclaimed.

"Oooooh! Is this one of your famous Not-Disgusting Fruit Cakes?" he asked, with a wicked gleam in his eye.

"Yes it is! I'll put it in the kitchen for you." After she carefully placed it in the middle of the counter where it was prominent and pretty, she took off her coat and walked back. "What are you working on today?" she asked.

"Just one second, Popcorn. I have to get it juuuuust… wait. Okay, that goes there, the transmitter and alternator…

Hmm… And Yep! Perfect." He often talked like that as he made adjustments to whatever project he was working on.

"Is it what I think it is, Reggie?" she asked excitedly.

"It sure is. I really think I have it! But we won't know for sure until tomorrow night. How's your dad? Did he sail already?" asked Mr. Fessenden, looking closely at her expression.

Poppy was taking her time to answer his question. She knew it was a simple question: Did her dad sail or not yet? But she was always honest with Mr. Fessenden and her feelings were very complicated with her father. So even a simple question had a lot that went with it. Mr. Fessenden was patient, letting her get her thoughts together.

"Yep. He sailed the day before yesterday. He'll be gone over Christmas. Again. I hate the Navy."

"Hmm," said Mr. Fessenden. "Yes, they can really mess up one's plans, can't they?" He kept tinkering with the dials and wires while watching her surreptitiously. "Poppy, are you alright?"

Poppy was shocked to hear her actual name. She wasn't sure he'd ever used her actual name before. "Well… I… I'm just not sure how to make my dad happy."

"You don't think he's happy?" he asked, trying to get her to unfold her thoughts.

"He doesn't seem to be. He's restless and unable to just sit and be with us. I don't know…" she said, tapping her temple while she mulled over the conundrum of her father. A few pesky crumbs fell out of her hair onto the table.

"Oh dear," she said. "He'd hate that. I can't seem to keep the crumbs from getting in my hair." She also noticed a splotch of blue paint on her thumb. How'd that get there?

Mr. Fessenden chuckled, "Oh, a few crumbs and paint smudges are evidence of a deep thinker, Sugar-pop. It means you are so brilliant, you can't be bothered with meaningless details."

Poppy wished her father felt the same way. But messiness was a cardinal sin to him. She worried that her father would never be able to see beyond her crumbs. Even worse, she didn't like the growing realization that their home was happier and not so full of tension when he was gone.

"Say, I have a question for you," declared Reginald in a tone that clearly declared a change in topic. "What is your favorite Christmas carol, Poppycock?"

"Oh, that's a difficult question. I like all of them. Well… Do I have to pick just one?"

"Yes."

Poppy held her chin and tapped it with a finger, imitating an aged professor. Reginald bit back a smile as he watched her.

"Alright. I have it. I'm not a fan of the opera, as you know." He nodded sagely, as Poppy always let everyone know what she didn't like. "But one time, there was this night time church service. My mother and father and I went to it together. I think I was really young, like five or six. But I remember it very clearly. At the beginning of the service, this tall, barrel-chested man came out on stage. In an incredibly deep voice, he sang *O Holy Night.* Oh my goodness. It raised the hairs on my arms and neck! It was haunting and so, so beautiful!"

She reflected on that night for a quick moment. She remembered being enthralled with that song, with the depth of the singer's voice. She had been holding her parents' hands on either side of her as they left the church service. She recalled trying to put into words everything she felt. It was so big, so much emotion, it'd been hard to find the right words. She wanted to see if her parents felt the same way. There was always something special about having someone really, truly understand the deep feelings you had. Like a favorite book that you find out your best friend has read a dozen times. You enjoy something incredible in the shared moment of discovery. But her dad had been consumed with the fact that it had been raining and his best shoes were getting wet. Poppy hadn't even noticed the rain. He hadn't heard one word she said. She looked at her mother and they shared a knowing look. Her mom squeezed her hand.

Maybe her dad would never understand her. Maybe… Maybe she shouldn't try anymore. Trying hard wasn't getting her anywhere. It was getting too hard. Because it meant too much.

"*O Holy Night* it is," he said, breaking into her thoughts.

"What is?" she asked, cocking her head to the side and wondering what he was up to.

"Oh you'll see. You and your mother be sure to turn on the radio I gave you, on Christmas Eve. Tomorrow night.

You'll have to ask her to let you stay up late. Until eleven. Okay?"

"Of course!"

"I have another idea. If your dad is at sea, perhaps we should try to send him a message. Would you like that? He'll have a Sparks on board of course. I'm sure a little telegraph message on Christmas Eve wouldn't hurt." Sparks was the name of all radio operators. Poppy was proud to be knowledgeable about such things.

"Uh… Well… That's all right. I wouldn't want to get my father in trouble."

"Are you sure? I'm sure he'd love a message from you…" he said, with a sad look in his eyes.

Her mind made up, she said, "No, that's okay. I'll give him his present in a couple days. It'll be fine. Oooh I'm so excited about your plans! I can't wait for Christmas Eve now!"

Poppy knew Mr. Fessenden received a lot of negative attention for his work with radios. People just didn't believe his ideas were possible. She wished they shared her own enthusiasm about his projects. But they would. After Christmas Eve.

Peter was on board his ship, off the coast of the United States, in the Atlantic. It was black outside, as he stood on deck, looking at utter darkness. It was cloudy, so no stars or moon were shining. The pitch of the ship lulled him and he always loved that feeling. It was now a part of him, as he found himself longing for it when he'd been on land too long. His cigar was almost at an end. He'd have to head in soon. The men had a party going on inside. It wasn't really what he wanted to do and if he went in for another cigar, he knew he'd be pulled into it. Oh well. It was getting very cold. He might as well go.

"Petey! Petey-Pete Peterson! Get in here and have some rum. I mean punch," slurred one of his buddies who had spiked the punch. He thought he was clever, secretly spiking it, but everyone knew. It made good ol' Geoffrey happier that way. "Petey, try shome."

"Hey there, Geoffrey, looks like you tried enough for me and the rest of the crew. But I'll take another cigar!"

"Heeeeeeeeeeere ya go! Take two," said Geoffrey with a flourish as he slid two big beautiful cigars out of his chest pocket.

"Thank you my man!" Peter stood over to the side, lit and puffed his cigar after pocketing the extra one. He looked around, taking it all in. Some guys had strung a few meager decorations around. Several families sent in cookies and desserts (the rum balls were the most coveted). And the Navy cooks were second-to-none. They didn't suffer when it wasn't wartime. There was a big roast beef being sliced up, mashed potatoes, rich dark brown gravy, some green thing that had to be a vegetable (he'd pass on that), and thick slices of bread that must've come out of the oven fresh because they were still steaming.

"Say Peter, you look sadder than a sad horse," exclaimed a gravelly voice next to him. Whitmore's booming voice surprised him. He thought he'd been happy looking around at all the friends and festivities. But apparently he didn't; you can't look sadder than a horse.

"I… I don't know, Whit." Whitmore sat down and motioned to Peter to sit down too. Whitmore was his oldest friend. They'd grown up together and even joined the Navy together. Some of the time they'd served apart, but the last two years they served on the same ships together. One side of Whitmore's right eyebrow still hadn't grown in from fighting the San Francisco fires. It gave him a quizzical look to an otherwise rugged and brawny guy. Whit was getting concerned about his missing eyebrow and would sometimes absently rub that spot as if he could magically make it regrow.

"Missin' something?" asked Peter with an evil chuckle.

"Grrrrrrrr," Whit growled. His fearsome growl once stopped a looting bunch of no-gooders at the wharf in San Fran right in their tracks, but his buddies knew he was all bark and no bite. So it had absolutely no effect on Peter. He just handed him one of his cigars. Mollified, Whit took it and got to the pleasing work of lighting it.

After a few minutes of companionable silence, Whitmore asked, "You looked as pleased as pleased could be when we boarded, Pete. Why all long in the face now?"

"Oh, just missing the family. You know how it is, Whit," he lied.

"Hm. Well, I sure know you boarded the ship with a smile. And I sure know after all these years that there hasn't been one Christmas that you enjoyed. Why is that?" asked Whitmore, taking a few puffs as he considered his friend.

Peter was very uncomfortable with this direct question. Whit wasn't being judgmental; he was the sort of guy who didn't have a judgmental bone in his body. It was an honest question. But Peter didn't really understand the answer himself. He stood there, arms crossed, shifting his weight from one foot to the other, trying to figure out how to answer.

"You know, Pete? You look just like your Grandpa right now." The two of them spent so much time together as kids, they both knew each other's relatives maybe even better than their own.

"You look like your grandma," countered Peter with a wry smile.

"Yeah. It's the lovely eyebrows," Whitmore said jokingly, waggling his bushy one-and-a-half brows at Peter.

They both barked out a laugh and took a couple of swigs of the punch, the rum warming their stomachs. "Hmm," reminisced Peter. "You really think I look like Grandpa Hutchins? I've been thinking about him a lot lately."

"You do. He was mostly happy, but there was a sadness in him. I could never understand what was behind it. He

92

kept those thoughts to himself, I guess," said Whitmore, shaking his head.

"That's funny you say that. God, I loved that man. He looked so innocent on the outside, but on the inside he was full of mischief," said Peter.

"Remember when we caught him with that magazine where the women's *ankles* were showing? At the time we thought that was something scandalous!" Whitmore's belly laugh was shaking the table next to them. It was a contagious guffaw and Peter joined in.

"And remember when Grandma Josephine got so mad at him when he decided to buy us all a big toboggan instead of the new sheets she'd asked him to purchase?" said Peter. "She'd been making pies when he came in all happy and ready to show us his big purchase. I thought she was going to hit him right over the head with that rolling pin in her hand. She'd drawn it back like she was giving it some serious thought."

"Ha ha ha!" Whitmore was wiping away the tears from laughing so hard.

Whit let Peter collect his thoughts. After a few moments Peter said, "You know? I was talking with Grandpa once, when I had to have only been ten or eleven. We were just talking about the day and I was excited because Christmas was coming soon." Whitmore's eyes darted to Peter's as he said this. Peter went on, "I started to ask him if Christmas was his favorite holiday, too. How could it not be? As a kid there are presents, good food, friends, Santa... What more could you want? But Grandpa said that his favorite holiday was Thanksgiving. I asked him why he felt that way. And he told me that Christmas brought up so many old memories that it made him sad. He missed the days when he was a kid and the family was all together."

"Huh. I thought he'd always had so much fun at Christmas," said Whitmore. That's... surprising. And a little... well, I guess I feel a little disappointed."

It was Peter's turn to shoot his eyes to Whitmore. "Really? I thought maybe I was just too sentimental. I always felt bad, too. It was such a great time for me; I wanted him to enjoy it just as much."

"More than that, it's a little hopeless, isn't it? I mean, I want Christmases in the years to come to be just as special as they are now," said Whitmore. "Maybe different, but still special."

"Yes! I started to worry that those fast years would be the best. That means no place to go but down from there." Whitmore nodded in complete understanding. "Everyone needs hope, I think. When you feel like nothing else will ever compare, it's just sad," said Peter. He took another thoughtful puff of his cigar. "But I don't know. Maybe he was right," said Peter. "Those Christmases as a kid were really wonderful."

"But Pete, don't you think enjoying Poppy at Christmas is even better? I can't get enough of little John and Ray. I never thought I'd like buying or making things more than I do for my sweetheart Mary, but the boys? It's so much fun. I've never seen so much joy in little things like wooden horses and that swing I made in the backyard. It was like I'd given them a castle!"

Peter took a good look at his friend Whitmore. Whit was smiling to himself, surely wishing he could be home with his wife and boys. Whit was completely in love with his wife, Mary. And he was crazy about his sons. He was right. Poppy's joy at the little doll Peter had brought her from San Francisco was so surprising to him. It filled him with total happiness. Funny that someone else's happiness could fuel your own.

Peter was getting closer to figuring it out. The missing piece to all this was coming within reach and it had to do with his grandpa's words. It made him feel excited.

"You look terrified," said Whitmore.

"Excited."

"No. Terrified."

"Alright, terrified. Excited, too," said Peter, compromising.

"Why?" chuckled Whit.

"Oh, just something I've been figuring out. Nothing to worry about. I'm going to go take a walk around deck."

"Okay! See you around, Pete. Thanks for the cigar!" he said with a smile, going back to rubbing his bald spot on his eyebrow.

Back out on deck, the wind was picking up strength. The pitch of the ship was stronger now and there was still no moon or starlight. The wind was changing; instead of southerly, it was from the east. It had a harshness to it when it came from the east. He decided to go see his friend, the radio operator on the bridge. See if a storm was brewing at sea.

"Hey Sparks!" he yelled. Sparks was a nickname for all the radio guys everywhere. But this Sparks was Neville. He was a tightly wound, sharp worker. His intense eyes were always looking off somewhere no one else could see, as he listened intently to the radio for Morse codes coming through. His hands were an extension of his alert mind. They flashed so quickly when he was sending his codes back across the air, they were a blur of action. It reminded Peter of a blind friend of his who could "read" the braille dots across his fingertips, as fast as eyes could see. It was miraculous to watch.

Neville must've needed a break because he leaned back more casually than Peter usually witnessed. "How are ya, Pete? Taking a walk?"

"Yup. Did you get some grub? The roast was excellent."

"I did! Thanks!" he said, rubbing his tight stomach. Everything about him was tight including his muscles. Wiry but extremely strong. He'd been a farmer with his folks growing up. There's no one stronger than a farmer.

"You missing your family, this fine Christmas Eve?" asked Peter.

"No, sir! There isn't anywhere I'd rather be than right here," he responded. Neville's mind was just as alert as his hearing and his fingers. He always knew what he wanted, and he could weigh the pros and cons of any situation almost instantly. He could make military decisions with deadly speed and accuracy. He'd be flying up the ranks of the Navy soon. The radio was his favorite thing, however.

"Why here?" asked Peter, genuinely curious.

"Well? Two things. There's nothing like being right here in the moment. You can never escape the tyranny of the moment, but you can be present. You can't go back, you can't go forward. So you'd better be happy with right now. Secondly…" he stopped with a slow grin growing across his face.

The first thing he'd said had practically stopped Peter's heart. *You can't go back, you can't go forward.* So… He had to chew on that. Then Neville was following up that right hook with a devilish grin? What was the man up to?

"What? What are you up to, Sparks?" asked Peter, squinting his eyes in concern.

"Oh, let's just say it's very interesting that you made your way up here at this precise moment. I was about to go find you. But here you are."

"You were going to go get me?" asked Peter in total surprise.

"You're not going to want to miss this."

"What's going on?"

"I don't know exactly," admitted Neville. "But I got a cryptic message over the wires from a call signal suspiciously near your own home. Brant Rock,

Massachusetts, right? And that you needed to be in the radio room at twenty-three hundred hours."

Peter's mind raced. It had to be that crazy neighbor of his. Poppy's friend. What was his name again? He started to tell Neville about the neighbor, dismissing the message. "Sorry, I mean, it was probably a joke or something. This neighbor of ours has a crazy workshop in his home, even a giant antennae coming out the top of the roof!"

Neville cut him off sharply with a raised arm. "Wait! What *exactly* is your neighbor's name?"

His menacing tone caught Peter off guard. "I, um. I think it was Reg... Reginald Fester?"

"Oh my god. Reginald Fessenden? Reginald Fessenden is your neighbor. *Your* neighbor, Pete?"

Peter nodded his head dumbly. "Yeah."

Neville suddenly shouted to the AB, the able seaman who assisted the OOW, the Officer of the Watch, as lookout, "Go get the Captain. Now! Now! Wait – don't scare him. It's not an attack, but he and the XO have to get up here. They won't want to miss this. Go!" The guy shot out of there, bounding down to get the officers, the OOW curious but not taking his eyes away from his watch.

"Sparks! What are you doing?" Peter was really worried now. "Are you all right? That message had to have been a joke! What are you doing?"

Despite the urgency of his voice, Neville's grin became even more devilish. "You, my friend, have no idea who your neighbor is. *I do*." Then he turned back to his dials and his headset, turning things and clicking buttons. As if to himself he started muttering, "I can't imagine. What is he going to do? What could this mean? Hmm. He couldn't have… No. No. Could he? Oh my God."

Peter started sweating. Neville was consumed in his own world and something about his crazy neighbor and God-forbid his own daughter was spooking the crew of a U.S. military destroyer. Good Lord. Footsteps came bounding up the stairs and then barged in to the bridge.

"What the sam hell is going on here?" boomed the Captain.

Both Neville and Peter stood up, saluting, "Sir, yes, sir!"

"At ease, and you better tell me what the devil is going on." The captain, XO and several other officers who saw the captain running full out had accompanied the group.

"Sir," began Neville. "Today I received a cryptic message from a neighbor of Sgt. Hutchins'. It said he had to be up here at twenty-three hundred. But he came up of his own accord."

The captain began spluttering, "What the devil? Pete's neighbor? For God-sakes!"

"Please, sir. His neighbor is *Reginald Fessenden*." Peter looked to the captain, unsure what to think. One of the other officers gasped, but the captain looked like Neville had just said he got a radio message from a snowman.

"If you took me from the only Christmas celebration I'm going to have, to hear some cockamamie story, you…"

"Wait! Wait! I just heard something. Hold on. Hold on," exclaimed Neville, turning the dials with exquisite precision. Whatever was happening, despite the bluster of the captain, the air had shifted. There was a tension of expectancy, like when you're waiting for the thunder to hit after you just saw a streak of lightning. The urgent whispers from the officer who understood the import of the name of Reginald Fessenden added to the tension as the whispers spread through the chain of men.

Suddenly, Neville's arm shot into the air. The whole room came to an abrupt halt; no one daring to breathe. His right arm trembled as he raised his index finger, shaking it like he was saying, *wait – wait for this.* Slowly he took off his headset, and reached up to the switch that would transmit what he was hearing in his headphones to the speakers throughout the room.

The captain tried one more splutter, "Man! We don't need to hear all those dees and dahs! Just tell us…" But as he said those words, Neville hit the switch.

Instead of the beeps and dees and dahs that they'd all been expecting to hear, for the first time ever in history… a voice erupted from the radio waves.

"And it came to pass in those days, that there went out a decree from Caesar Augustus, that all the world should be taxed…" A voice. A real, human voice! No one had ever heard anything over the radio except nondescript sounds. Ever. And suddenly there was a voice from over the ocean, speaking as if by magic into their bridge. The voice continued with the second chapter of Luke, telling of the Christ child's birth. "…And the angel said unto them, Fear not; for, behold, I bring you good tidings of great joy, which shall be to all people. For unto you is born this day in the city of David a Saviour, which is Christ the Lord. And this shall be a sign unto you; Ye shall find the babe wrapped in swaddling clothes, lying in a manger. And suddenly there was with the angel a multitude of the heavenly host praising God, and saying, Glory to God in the highest, and on earth peace, good will toward men."

Then there was a bit of silence and the men all stood there, looking at each other with wonder and awe. Peter was astounded. It was a miracle. They all knew they were part of something amazing. He looked out on those black waters, feeling the up and down, up and down, of the ship. He breathed in, and appreciated that moment.

Then, before any of them moved a muscle, so caught up in the wonder of it all, another sound came through. Low and eerie, a sound full of the tune of long years past, the sound that was the backdrop of countless human moments… A *violin*. It was a sound he'd never forget in an eternity of years. The strains of *O Holy Night* ebbed and flowed across the Atlantic, over the waves, through the changing winds, under the velvet sky, and into their ship. Into their souls.

Neville was grinning from ear to ear, shaking his head in fascination. He looked at the captain and the other officers. All of them had been caught up in the moment. More than a couple of the sea-hardened men were wiping tears from their eyes.

Most importantly, however, Peter had found that last piece of the puzzle he'd been searching for. In fact, it was the piece he'd been looking for, ever since he was ten years old and had that chat with his grandfather. He knew what to do.

❧

Christmas morning, Poppy awoke to the scent of cinnamon and vanilla wafting through the house. Her mother made an oatmeal that simmered on the stove for hours. She laced it with heavy cream and then a sprinkling of milk chocolate. It was ridiculously delicious. And there was something special about having that scent to wake up to, another part of the day that wrapped her in a blanket of happiness. She heard the sweet sounds of cooking and dishes being cleaned up in the kitchen, a coffee cup being set down. But wait! There were two cups in succession that had been set down. She knew it immediately. Her mind had been subconsciously hunting for that sound. The sound that meant another person was in the kitchen besides her mother.

Maybe Reggie had dropped by? She'd never forget that Christmas Eve as long as she lived. The only thing that could have topped it, would be if she'd been able to be out somewhere far away, somewhere lonely, where the only sounds over the radio were the dees and dahs of the telegraph. Ooh, if only she could've been in that exact spot where the sounds of Reggie's haunting violin stretched out and met her! That would've been wonderful; a moment that you'd look back on and know you'd been a part of history.

Her feet dropped to the cold floor, sending shivers up and down her body. She quickly grabbed her robe and put it over her long nightgown with the pretty lace at the bottom, where her toes peeked out. Then she stuffed those toes into the fleece slippers her father had brought her once, all the way from Maine. Feeling secure and snug and ready for that oatmeal, not to mention the moment she'd get to see the Christmas tree and presents, she took a deep breath. Poppy didn't want to miss out on one little detail of this special day.

Poppy suddenly missed her father. She knew she would, but quite honestly, there had been a small part of her that was relieved he'd be gone. She had decided maybe she shouldn't try so hard with him. Maybe she'd stop trying to unlock the secret, unrevealed man that he was. She just would never understand him and vice versa. She hated to even admit it to herself! She felt awful for feeling that way, but he would be upset with the wrappings from the presents lying all over the place. And he'd be looking at her hair, with the crumbs inevitably in there. She hated those crumbs, too, but try as she might, when she was consumed with making an art project or reading a good book, she just didn't realize what her hands were doing! So maybe it would be easier without her dad just for this day of big messes. She'd make up for these thoughts tomorrow when he got home, by trying hard to be extra neat. She'd do her best to make him happy.

She skipped out to the kitchen, stopped dead in her tracks, and then almost fell over from surprise. Her dad was standing at the stove stirring the oatmeal, which he had obviously made himself. The reason she knew this was because he had spilled – yes, spilled – the oatmeal on the counter along with a few chocolate pieces. *And left them there.* There were even a couple of pieces on his bare feet.

She must've made some sort of noise because her mother who'd been sitting at the table with her coffee looked over at her and said cheerily, "Merry Christmas, Sweetheart!"

Her dad stopped stirring the oatmeal and put his hands on his hips with the biggest, most *revealing* smile she'd ever seen on him. "Poppy? I got your message."

"Wh… What message?" she whispered. She'd never sent him a message.

"You might not have realized you sent me a message, but I received it loud and clear."

"What are you talking about?" she asked.

"I can hardly describe it!" he exclaimed. "We were all on the ship last night and my friend Sparks got a message from our neighbor. I had no idea he was the radio genius that had been changing the world."

Poppy could hardly speak. For one, she was outraged because she had indeed told her father about Reginald many times. Secondly, she had specifically told Reggie to not give her dad a message. "But what message?" she asked.

"Well, Sparks said it just told him to make sure that I was in the radio room at eleven; that I wouldn't want to miss out on something really special. But then, he figured out the sender was Reginald Fessenden and suddenly he's barking out orders to get the captain and the officers!"

Poppy got a little scared. What had Reginald done? Was it bad that he figured out how to speak over the radio waves?

"Oh don't worry, Poppy," said her father quickly, seeing the apprehension on her face. "It's okay, the captain wouldn't have missed it for the world."

"Really?" she asked.

"Yes! So we were all standing together, about twenty of us all crammed onto the bridge, and suddenly we heard… words! Human words! I can't even try to express how shocked we all were. And then… Then the violin! It was like we were in another world. And it was the same song we heard at that late night Christmas service one year. Remember?"

Poppy and her mother looked at each other and shared a secret, knowing smile. Her dad kept going, unable to stop, "Those notes are so haunting. So remarkable. And then to have that sound reach out like that, to all of us so far out in the ocean, and it was so dark. And then the music. The music!" He sat down with a plop onto the kitchen chair, unable to properly say all he wanted to say.

Poppy knew exactly how that felt. She dove in with a joy she couldn't remember ever having before. "Dad! I understand! It was like you were in a cold, lonely place and untouchable. Then the music reached your heart in ways that you didn't even know were possible! Oh I wish I had been there so badly!"

Her father looked stunned. "Exactly, Poppy. You *do* understand," he said with a smile. "It was like… It was like magic. I never wanted it to stop."

It was her turn to be stunned. It was delicious. Her heart was full because she could finally share what she longed to share with her father. That night with the opera singer had been incomplete because she'd so desperately wanted her father to be involved in the wonder of it all. And she had wanted to be on that ship, hearing the violin over the radio for the first time in history. Her father at last let her in, to share in that spectacular moment. A weight had been lifted off her shoulders, and the relief was delightful. She sighed, feeling content and happy.

"Daddy," she said, an impish grin growing ear to ear on her face. "Clean up that oatmeal! And that chocolate on your feet! Clean that up, mister!" she exclaimed in a fair impression of his usual clean-it-up voice.

At that her mother could contain herself no longer. A completely unladylike guffaw barked out of her mouth, "Hah hah hah!" Then she broke down into giggles absolutely worthy of an eight-year-old. In fact, her motherly face turned into a much younger version of itself as her infectious laughter filled the old kitchen.

Poppy dissolved into giggles as well and then they both stopped abruptly as a wad of wax paper popped off the top of her mother's head. Her father had thrown it at her.

Her mother was stunned, her mind completely unable to discern what had happened. And then another piece ricocheted off of Poppy's head. He did it again!

Peter was apparently so pleased with his actions that his own mischievous grin revealed the eight-year-old within, too. His ridiculous actions had his wife and daughter completely frozen, and he seemed to think he should take advantage of the situation. He picked up the oven mitt and kitchen towel and threw them at them. Poppy and her mother as a team instantly picked up the mitt and two of the wax paper balls and threw them right back, one smacking his ear and the mitt popping him right in the nose.

"Oh I am going to get you both!"

A wonderful race, tickle, and throwing fight happened all over their little home filling every room with laughter.

❧

Poppy knew deep in her heart that her father had received her message in more ways than she even understood. And Peter finally came to terms with the fact that he could never hold back the imminent nature of change. But he could control the fear of it. The best way to take that fear by the reins, was to master the enjoyment of the moment. There was nothing he could do about the future. But there was everything he could do about the present. He chose to be there. And to soak up every detail.

CHAPTER 8

I exhaled happily and then popped the last piece of a dainty little pink macaron into my mouth while I thoughtfully looked at the woman sitting before me. Mrs. Foxmorten had grown increasingly serene as she shared Poppy and Peter's story. Her recall for details was uncanny and she had a lilting, funny way of voicing the dialog that made them all the more charming. At first, she had been silly and closing in on absurd. But now, she was calm and collected.

"How did you say you know this story so well, with so many vivid details, Mrs. Foxmorten?" I asked, dying to know. I couldn't remember what she'd said when we met.

"Oh, I heard the tale from Poppy."

"*The* Poppy?" I exclaimed.

"Actually, this Poppy's daughter. Poppy loved her name, you see, so she named her first daughter Poppy, too. I was her daughter's best friend growing up." We'd just said *Poppy* about a billion times. "It was our favorite story. I'd spend the night over there and we'd beg and beg for her to tell us the story! Even the parts about the earthquake. That was exciting. Of course, when we were little she didn't tell us all the scary or more serious bits. But as we grew up, she'd reveal more. Then when we were old enough, she even let us read some of the articles about the earthquake and fire as well as the radio wave sensation. You know, Reginald had another radio transmission on New Year's Eve that supposedly reached as far as the Caribbean. I just don't think we can understand how momentous that was," she said wistfully.

I agreed. This assignment was a funny one. Some just are. Some take arduous work to dig and find sources, while others just seem to come together like a well-used puzzle. You know how all the parts fit together because you've done it a hundred times, and it's so satisfying to see it come together so well and so quickly. This one was like that. Like the stars aligned and I was getting not only the right people to talk to, but they were fabulous storytellers. I think it was because each of them cared so deeply about the topic. It had somehow become a part of their own story. Which is always the most compelling.

Along these lines, I wasn't half surprised when she said, "I have a friend you have to talk to!"

In fact, she called her friend right then and there and set up an immediate appointment. We walked out of the Bosie together and she pretty much shoved me into a cab, she was so enthusiastic. As she gave me a push, literally on my butt as I got into the cab, she yelled, "You'll just love Father Espinoza! He's eager to meet you, too!" I motioned through the closed window that I couldn't hear her, which I easily could, just to get her to yell even louder. I had fun.

I got out of the cab early so I could walk north along the Hudson River. I was coming up to Chelsea Piers, a big athletic facility. My mouth fell open as I walked past a couple of people learning how to use a trapeze. They were about 25 feet off the ground and I couldn't hold back a squeal as a woman let go of the trapeze and fell into the huge net with a swoosh. So… Not just batting cages and bowling here. Alrighty then.

I was thinking about Poppy and her relationship with her father. I liked that Peter had learned about enjoying the moment. I needed to learn a little about that myself. Especially when I was eating salt-less potatoes. I laughed to myself. I still felt like I was looking for something. Kind of like Peter looking for that piece of the puzzle that he was missing. And also a little antsy like Tom Murphy when he was being prodded to buy that first Christmas tree for Rockefeller Center. I think I was beginning to find the answers I was looking for. It was partly this city, too. I really felt at home here. Awake and alive.

I needed to share it with someone. I got out my phone and texted my brother Jim.

"Having a LOT of fun. How are you?"

I waited impatiently but was then rewarded by the little dots that tell you someone's writing you back.

"Great! Can't wait to hear about it! So you're not Scrooge after all. Hah! I knew it."

"Shut up Jimmy☺"

"Never."

"I'll call you later. I love New York. Wish you were here!"

"Love you, Christmas Journalist. TTYL"

I love my brother. He's awesome. I felt better having shared that quick text, too. Poppy was right. It's more fun when you can share what you're really excited about.

Within a couple of blocks I found the General Theological Seminary of the Episcopal Church. Father Espinoza, just like Billy and Mrs. Foxmorten, was obviously eager to tell me his story. I knew this because he was waiting outside, fairly bobbing on his toes in excitement.

Father Michael Espinoza was a bright-eyed and bushy-tailed 50-year-old. He looked about 30 except for the crinkles around his eyes and a little gray around his temples. He was not a conventionally good-looking man, but his spirit was utterly joyful and I felt lifted up when I shook his hand. He was a very positive, alive person.

"I can hardly believe my luck that Mrs. Foxmorten called me and I was in today! I am usually all over the place and have so many meetings. But today must be special. Everything is turning out right." Boy did he hit the nail on the head. And I was enjoying myself more than I had on any other assignment. I felt like I knew these people from the past, and I cared about them like they were my friends. I was learning so much.

"Come! Let us walk and talk. The High Line is beautiful," he said with a nod to where we'd take the stairs up to a walkway.

"Wonderful! I really appreciate you taking the time to meet with me," I said as we started to climb.

"Your story sounds very interesting. Mrs. Foxmorten was most excited when she called me," he said with a grin.

"I bet," I said knowingly.

He chuckled, "Yes. She yelled so loudly I dropped my phone."

"You should have heard her at the Bosie Tea Shop!" I said, laughing.

"She does not lack enthusiasm, does she?"

"No. She most certainly does not," I said.

I was enjoying looking around. The High Line was a park and walkway that had transformed old, unused elevated train tracks. Hundreds of people were milling around, enjoying the green space. There were sculptures, benches, and trees all beautifully woven together. Being up off the ground gave it this interesting feel that other parks don't have. I heard many languages and smelled good food from various vendors. Up ahead the Freedom Tower reached to the sky along with several other unusual buildings that might have been apartments.

After we strolled a while, Father Espinoza said, "I have a story to tell about how Christmas stockings came to be a tradition."

I was excited. My parents didn't *do* Santa, so we obviously didn't have stockings. But I'd always harbored a secret wish for a filled stocking by the fire. I love the idea of tiny gifts in a stocking. Especially in the toe. Maybe... Maybe I'd make a stocking for my brother Jim this year. We always had Christmas Eve dinner with our parents, but we'd share a cocktail, just the two of us ahead of time. I could give it to him then. That would be really fun. And if I ever had kids, I'd love to do things like that...

"Jane?" Father Espinoza said, touching my elbow. "Where'd ya go?" he asked playfully.

"Oh! Sorry! I got ahead of myself and started thinking about stockings and how I'd write my story..." I was making this up as I went.

He was smirking at me.

"Why are you smirking?" I asked bluntly, trying hard not to smile.

"You are an interesting person, Jane Smith," he said, considering me as we walked.

"I am?" That was not what I thought he'd say.

"Yes. You are. I think I will enjoy getting to know you." I was very pleased by this.

"So how did you come to know this story you're about to tell me?" I asked.

"I had been researching the early church in the area that is now Turkey, for a class I was teaching. This particular story goes all the way back to the 4th century and Saint Nicholas. His family had been extremely wealthy, but both parents died young. They left him their fortune and he used it to give to the poor. He was very innovative in how he gave his gifts. I'd read many variations of the story of how stockings became a tradition. But the one I'm going to tell you about, I found documented in a very old book I discovered when I was traveling in Turkey. It was in the cathedral library where the story supposedly takes place. The little volume wasn't original to the 4th century, but close! It had been copied judiciously by the scribes and was from the 6th century. It was a tiny little thing, about the size of my phone. I had to be very careful as I handled it.

"There are many renditions of this story; it is one of the most prevalent of Saint Nicholas' adventures. Only the Lord knows if this telling is the truest one, but it certainly is the dearest. And it goes far, far beyond what we know of the stockings today. It all began with a poor and starving widower and his three daughters.

CHAPTER 9

Myra, Turkey
351 A.D

Every night she pulled off her stockings, dark and stinky with dirt and grime from the long, hard day of trying to find work. If she did find work, it was the dirtiest, most disgusting kind of work. Because no one else wanted to do it. But she'd happily do it. It meant not starving for one more day. And one day at a time was all they could plan. They were all holding on by a thread.

Besides, she didn't deserve any better. She gladly did the work. It was penance.

Rebekkah scrubbed the stockings, trying to get the dirt and grime off while also trying not to harm her only set of stockings. She'd already darned them a dozen times. Her right foot had a few blisters from the darns that she'd made. It couldn't be helped. New stockings cost an unthinkable fortune when all the money in the house bought a single loaf of bread and maybe an onion or a potato.

She went to bed the same way she went to bed every night: in between her two sisters, hungry, and listening to the snores of her father, wishing upon wish she'd never left this miserable bed that one night. That horrible night that changed her forever. Guilt and grief were burdensome companions, so she drifted off to sleep to escape for several hours. Then she'd start all over again the next day.

The following evening, Rebekkah and her sisters were tidying up their little home before they'd go to bed for the night. They heard raised voices outside and they shot one another wary glances. Rebekkah was the oldest at 18, so she reached out and patted the littlest sister on the top of the head. "Don't worry Lydia, you just keep cleaning, I'll see what it is. I can hear Papa's voice, so he must be arguing with the landlord again."

"All right, Rebekkah," she replied in her high voice, continuing to sweep.

Francine, the middle sister, held her arm before she went out the door and whispered, "Be careful, Rebekkah. Don't get too close. He's mean."

Rebekkah tried to cast off their concern, "Oh don't worry so much. He's all bluster. I'll just go see if I can listen in."

Despite her own words, Rebekkah's heart was pounding as she closed the door cautiously behind her. She crept to the side of the shack they called home and peered into the night. It wasn't in fact the landlord, it was one of Papa's friends. She didn't particularly like this man. He was nice enough to them, but in a way that seemed false. He reminded her of a weasel, continually looking for a way to take advantage of a good opportunity. And he always smelled sour. Her father's voice was strained and he was trying to keep his composure while keeping his voice as low as possible. But it wasn't very possible. She could hear his hoarse reply to what his friend had just suggested.

"I will not prostitute my own daughters, man!" Rebekkah's hand flew to her mouth, holding in a cry as much as her revulsion.

"But you're starving! Look at you, with your bones poking out and your face all yellow and drawn. Think of the greater good! You can't afford a dowry for any of them and you're all going to die! You just said that your littlest was sick last month. What will it take? All three of them dying? Just sacrifice one of them and save the other two! Or... I heard there's a way to sell them."

Her father almost choked, "Sell...? How could I...?"

"A life of slavery is better than dying in this wretched place, watching each other die right along with!" The dirty, sweaty man spat on the ground; he was so disgusted at her father's obvious blindness to the dire situation.

"Don't you think my heart aches every single night, every day, every hour, for the life I cannot give my daughters? If I could only sell myself, I'd do it in a moment! I can't afford the dowry that's required so they could escape this place."

Rebekkah's own heart ached as she watched her father rub the back of his neck, searching for some sort of solution. She wished that her mother was still alive. They could certainly use her wisdom right then. She had insisted the girls learn to read and write, practically a criminal offense to most men, but her father agreed. He had never learned to read himself, and he knew the girls would be better able to protect and provide for themselves if they could read. Her mother found a young apprentice who was willing to teach Rebekkah whenever his schedule would permit; then she taught the others. The family's situation hadn't been quite so dire back then, but Rebekkah's teacher, Stephen, never charged them for his lessons.

The man made one last jab at her father, "You are a worthless father and a worthless man. I shouldn't have wasted my time trying to tell you the right thing to do. You'll be the reason you all die." He spat on the ground again and stomped away; leaving both Rebekkah and her father rooted to the spot, the horror of the situation too strong, too miserable to comprehend.

Rebekkah's hand was still clamped over her mouth, not trusting herself not to make a sound. Her heart was breaking. It should be her. She should just offer herself to sell. She deserved no better and maybe it would help her sisters and her father get out of this hardship.

There was only one person she could trust with this decision. But she'd have to reveal everything. *Everything.* Otherwise he wouldn't understand why it should be her that should be sold. She quietly walked back to their home and gently crept into bed, trying not to wake her sisters, who had given up on finding out what was going on outside. They were sound asleep, looking innocent and peaceful. Rebekkah wished with every ounce of her being that she looked like that when she slept. She highly doubted it.

The next morning, Rebekkah stood outside the chapel, waiting for her teacher to come out. She wanted to wait until he was gone, so she could talk to the Bishop by herself. *If* she could find the courage. He would understand her situation and maybe help her find a good place to sell herself into slavery. It sounded ludicrous, but she had no idea how to go about figuring this out.

As soon as Stephen came out, she would go in to see the Bishop and get it over with. Stephen was such a good man and a patient, interesting teacher. She liked how his curly dark hair fell onto his brow and he kept swiping it back, trying to get it to stay. It never did. He was about 25 years old, much older than her 18 years. He'd been married a few years back, but his wife had died giving birth to their first child. As did the child. Maybe that's what made him seem so much older than she was. He was a serious sort of person, but when he smiled, it just felt good to be around him.

She waited for what seemed like hours and finally she steeled herself to just go into the chapel to find the Bishop; perhaps Stephen had left already. She wiped her nervous, sweaty hands on her skirt and went inside. And ran right into someone.

She felt two strong hands steadying her shoulders and looked up expecting it to be Stephen.

"B-b-Bishop Nicholas! I'm so sorry…" she stuttered.

The newly-named Bishop looked into Rebekkah's eyes and a kind smile stretched across his face, making his eyes crinkle. "Rebekkah, I hear you're one of Stephen's pupils, aren't you?" he asked.

She felt a blush creep up her neck. It was not typical for women to learn to read. So many people frowned upon it, she'd learned to just not talk about it. Rebekkah was utterly shocked that the Bishop knew about it. And was smiling.

"Uh… yes, I am," she said, just above a whisper.

His eyes saw something in her face. His brow wrinkled with concern and he cocked his head to the side.

"Rebekkah," he said. She was pretty sure she had never heard her name spoken, really spoken, that way before.

"Yes?"

"Are you carrying something burdensome, child?"

"Well, I... I think I am. Yes," she said, completely flummoxed at this direct question.

"Would you like to tell me about it? Maybe I can help you carry it."

It sounded so simple. She wanted to keep her family's misery a secret, but with the Bishop, maybe it was all right to share. So she did. They sat down on a little bench right there, and she told him all about her father's dilemma, their situation, and how they didn't have a loaf of bread to their name. She tried to not complain, just told him the facts. Then she even revealed her plan to sell herself. She expected him to be mortified.

But when she finished, he pursed his lips together and cocked his head to the side again and said, "Hmm. That would solve your financial issues for at least a little while. But something bothers me. That would be quite a sacrifice, on your part. Yet you never talked about sacrifice, you said that you deserved no better. Why did you say that, daughter?" he asked gently.

Rebekkah had told herself so many times that she didn't deserve any better, that she hadn't realized she'd actually used those words with the Bishop. She felt trapped and naked. She looked down as her face was turning red with shame and she felt a familiar lump in her throat. She stole a glance up at the Bishop, expecting… Well, she didn't know what to expect. But what she saw was unexpected. His dark eyes were warm with compassion. She didn't like that. She wanted judgment. So she told him. He'd understand then, how selling herself wouldn't be a sacrifice; it would be penance.

She felt the Bishop watching her carefully as a wide range of emotions flowed through her: fear, regret, deep pain, and seething anger.

"You don't understand! Don't look at me with compassion, I don't deserve it. And I'll prove it."

She took a deep breath and started to relentlessly share her story. The story that was the root of the burden she was carrying. She'd had it. She just couldn't stay quiet. It was right that she bare her soul. "I'm not innocent! I just… About a year ago, there was a man new to our village. And I…"

She was stuck for words. The Bishop asked, "Did he seduce you?"

Her eyes popped up to his, a little surprised he even knew and could say that word. In a church. "No! That's the problem. I went to *him*. And we lay together. I thought, I thought that I wanted to be with him. I… And then afterward he laughed. He laughed at me! And then he left. Left the village," said Rebekkah, throwing her arms up in exasperation.

"Did you want him as a husband?"

"No! And that's the problem, too! I mean, I heard the sermon at church about the woman who had a horrible husband and she's had to deal with him all these years. I've heard about the man whose wife wasn't faithful and how he fared. How that one woman's husband beats her when he's drunk. Well... Everyone has to deal with the awful people in their life. But I *am* the horrible person! I'm the one who didn't have prostitution forced on me, I *chose* it! I didn't do something wrong out of oppression, I chose evil because I just wanted it!"

She stopped, having unloaded everything. There, she thought. *Now* he'll judge. Good. She could get on with paying for it. Rebekkah looked up at him, her arms crossed defiantly across her chest.

The Bishop sat there looking at her, his hands clasped casually in front of him, nodding his head. "Yes. I understand. Jesus's lineage is cow manure, too."

"Wh... *What*?"

"Mm hm. Full of evil-choosers such as yourself. Such as myself. Mm hm. Rahab, great-grandmother of King David was a prostitute. Abraham was a liar. Jacob a cheat. David was a murderer and adulterer. Moses whined frequently not to mention he murdered a man. Most of Jesus' followers were the dregs of society. In fact the woman who was probably his most devout follower was a prostitute and full of demons. Her name would be forever linked with evil, *Mary Magdalene the one who'd been possessed. Mary Magdalene, the grievous sinner...* But Jesus, Jesus called her *Mary*. And he chose her to be the first to witness him

122

raised from the dead, and to be the messenger to the others that he had conquered death."

The way the Bishop said the name *Mary*, made her shiver. She could easily think of Jesus saying it the same way. Honest, fully knowing, but also fully loving.

"Rebekkah," he said, taking her hand in his, "You do not deserve to be sold as a slave, child. You are the daughter of a king, even if you don't feel like you are. You are valuable because you are His. And all of us are horrible people, as you say. If God's forgiveness is good enough for King David, and Moses, and Mary of Magdala, and Peter and John... It is good enough for you. It is time you forgive yourself." Then he took one last look at her, smiled largely, and said, "Be sure to continue your lessons. You might be one of the only women in all of Asia Minor able to read." Then he muttered to himself as he walked away, "Honestly. Not worthy. Ridiculous."

Rebekkah was rooted to the spot. A delicious feeling of freedom was beginning to spread through her. She felt lighter than... Well maybe ever. She was quiet, enjoying the peacefulness of the sanctuary. It was like she was in another world, it was so quiet. None of the sadness or pressures or fears could reach her in here.

She heard a slight shuffle behind her, over by the hallway off to the side. She thought maybe it was the Bishop returning. She ran over to the corner, hoping to tell him how thankful she was for his kindness. She rounded the corner and everything she'd been experiencing shattered to the ground. Standing there, obviously having overheard every word she and the Bishop had shared, was Stephen.

"No!" she whispered, unbelievably crushed to know that he'd heard of her shame, her embarrassment, and then even her humility and desperation over their family situation. She knew he'd probably known that part, but it's one thing to think it, and a completely different thing to hear her speak of it.

He obviously felt awkward, too. "I just… I walked out of the hall, then I heard voices and I turned back, but the door closed shut and locked! I didn't know what to do. I'm so sorry," said Stephen.

She felt all the color drain out of her face. "You heard? You heard everything?" she whispered.

He wanted to deny it, but his honest face wasn't capable of subterfuge. She didn't know what to do. She wasn't a fainter. Her one friend worked on the art of fainting to get out of tricky situations. Rebekkah wanted to cry, but then again she was so sick and tired of feeling disgusted about it all. So the tears didn't come. Half of her wanted to punch him.

He must have seen these emotions race across her face, especially the punching part, because he said, "Uh… Whoa, there," like you would to a horse about to rear up.

She took a second to consider. Then she looked again at his face. Took a good, long look. Something about him changed. He paused, slowly letting his arms settle down to his sides, letting her look. Unafraid. Unashamed. They stood there a long time. What surprised her was what she didn't see. She didn't see embarrassment on his part. Nor did she see disgust or pity. That was confusing to her.

Suddenly, he cocked his head to the side, not unlike the Bishop had just done moments before. And he said, "I have an idea. I want to show you something."

Completely taken unawares, she agreed. "All right."

They walked for quite a ways without saying a word. But it was a nice silence. Companionable. After all the emotions that were spent in the cathedral, Rebekkah was running short of anything other than simply enjoying the peace that had invaded her spirit. The relief was like having an illness for a long, long time and one day, waking up to find that it was over. The illness had run its course and was gone. It was freeing, and enabled her to see little things and gain enjoyment from them. Little things, like the tiny yellow flowers on the floor of the woods they were walking through at the far end of their village. They started climbing up a grassy hill. The birds chirped cheerily and the grass's scent was earthy and sweet. Up ahead was an outcropping of rocks and Stephen climbed up, and then held out his hand to her.

Other than her father, no man had ever held out his hand to her. His eyes were deep blue and endlessly kind. She took his hand, making him smile. He helped her up to the top and then they sat and enjoyed the view. It looked out over a rolling valley. The sun kissed the little hills and they could see the village, horses going to and fro, and every once in a while, they could hear children playing some sort of game, cheering each other on.

"It's beautiful," she said.

"It is, isn't it?" said Stephen, as he pulled up his knees and wrapped his arms around them.

Rebekkah started to wonder why he'd brought her out here and self-consciously pulled a stray piece of her hair behind her ear. She looked down at her only dress. It was so gray, with so many patches. She'd love to have a new dress.

Stephen turned to her and said bluntly, "I admit that I heard pretty much everything that you and the Bishop were saying." Then they both decided to look out at the view again. "And I want you to know, I'm not a good person either."

He said it with such heartfelt sincerity, it absurdly made her laugh. He was such a good person, it sounded ridiculous to hear him say otherwise. "I'm sorry! I shouldn't laugh."

He looked at her with mock anger, "You don't believe that I'm not good?"

"Not for one instant," said Rebekkah, shaking her head.

"Hmph. Well. I am not. Whether or not you believe it." He sighed. "And I've made choices I regret, as well. Things I wish I could change, Rebekkah." He turned to her then, and looked right at her. Her laughter died; his eyes became solemn. And indeed, regret burned deep in those dark blue eyes.

He looked away from her and shook his head slowly, almost angrily. "I didn't want the baby."

She made a small gasp, and he looked at her. Fear rippled through his eyes, making her wonder if he thought she would be repulsed by his admission. But she only felt surprise. No judgment.

He exhaled, and went on, "I knew we'd married very young. And I was just starting to be able to provide for us. I didn't think I could support three of us. So when I found out my wife was pregnant, I was less than happy. Rebekkah, I was *not* kind, I was *not* happy about it. And I let her know. Even when I saw that she was crushed, I just couldn't let go of being angry. It was ludicrous. I was an idiot." He spat the words out, disgusted with himself. "By the end of the pregnancy, I'd come around a bit. I could see the baby moving and the beginning of what being a father could feel like. But it wasn't enough. I think I'd broken her heart. And then… they both died. Everything was suddenly gone. My hopes. My fears. My joy. God! I was such a fool!"

Rebekkah didn't really know what to do. She'd never seen him like this, but she wasn't afraid. She'd seen a lot in her young life. And she knew he didn't need her to say anything. So she just put her hand out and touched his arm, her thumb gently rubbing back and forth. After a few minutes of silence, listening to the birds chirp, the leaves rustling as the wind brushed against them, he put his hand over hers. Their eyes met, and they shared that deep understanding that only two people who've shared a dark part of their heart and somehow got through the muck and mire together, can understand.

"Let me tell you what my father told me a couple of years ago," he said. "Do you see that beautiful young forest right there? Over next to the large hill?"

"Oh yes," she said. "That's my favorite. The leaves are greener and the heather is like a soft, lavender blanket all around. It's the most beautiful part."

"It is, isn't it?" he said, contemplatively. Their hands were still touching, completely going against convention. Their fingers would move just the slightest bit, in a gentle caress that would send shivers up her spine. Rebekkah thought it was the most intoxicating thing she'd ever felt.

He smiled a little as he looked out at the forest. "Well, my father told me it was burned in a raging fire when he was a child. I think he had a part in that fire, to be honest, but he never said. There was a sadness in him that looked a lot like guilt. But by the time he was telling me the story, this wood had grown up from the ashes. I'll never forget his face as he told the story to me. He looked like he was seeing the woods for the first time. He was half talking to himself, and half talking with me. That morning, the rays of the sun broke through the clouds in a strong line, almost like a bolt of lightning. It was incredibly beautiful. There were birds everywhere, flowers coming up in earnest in those early summer months, squirrels flitting about, you could smell the pine and the honeysuckle… He'd tried to tell me what it had looked like when it was burnt and black, but he couldn't do it. He'd stop and start, but was only able to get out a word or two. It was the only time I ever saw him moved like that."

Rebekkah took this in. She looked harder at the woods, trying to see the evidence that it had been burned, she supposed. Stephen saw her looking intently. He said, "Can you tell it was burned, Rebekkah?"

"I really can't," she said hopefully.

"I can," he said. Her hopes that had been rising, suddenly crumpled. She looked down again, knowing she herself would be marked for life. She felt the weight of tears starting to gather on her eyelashes.

She felt a soft finger touch her chin and turn her face toward him. She slowly lifted her eyes to look directly in his, steeling herself for that judgment she'd been craving, but that now scared her more than she could bear. "I can tell, because I had a talk with the Bishop, too. I'll never forget it. I confessed everything; about not wanting the baby, about wondering if I'd killed them by my own selfish wishes, about being an idiot and regretting it all." He laughed a contemplative sort of laugh, "He gave me the same lineage of Jesus speech. I'd carried that... *burden* for so long. Yet it suddenly lifted. And I could start again." Stephen looked directly at her. "Rebekkah, I can tell the wood was burned because it's stronger and more beautiful *now*. Rebekkah, there is greatness and beauty when something is rebuilt, overcoming seemingly impossible obstacles. It's... breathtaking."

Rebekkah slowly rested her head against his shoulder, letting out a deep sigh that she'd been holding in for a year, smiling and yet feeling the weight of those tears trickle down her cheek. They stayed silent, breathing in the air laced with the hope of summer. She felt a kiss on the top of her head. Nothing in her life had ever felt so good.

That night, she lay in her bed, surrounded by her sisters. She had no idea how things would work out with their dire situation. They were still hungry. Her father was still grieved. But it was the first time in her life she prayed, she really prayed. Not a prayer of request, she'd done plenty of that, but one of thanks. And she knew, she told Him that she knew He'd provide for them. Somehow. She thanked Him, because no matter what happened, she'd be forever grateful for this day of reckoning, of hope, and of forgiveness.

❧

Many hours later, after the sisters and the father were in their beds sound asleep, a shadowy figure crept by the window. He was stealthy, not wanting to wake them and having a childish joy for surprises. Nicholas didn't exactly know how he was going to go about doing this. He had an idea for this family. If anyone needed a spark of wonder and joy, it was they. Oh he could hardly contain himself thinking about the next morning! He thanked the Lord over and over again for giving him a family who had enjoyed wealth, so that he could secretly, joyously spread it around.

Hmm. But how to do it? He couldn't just leave the gold by the door, it'd be stolen in about three minutes. He looked at the shabby little hovel, as neat as neat could be, but still shabby. There was smoke coming out of the chimney so he couldn't throw it up there and he surely wasn't going to climb up there. He peeked in the window, hoping none of them would suddenly wake and be scared out their minds to see a stranger peeking in. He saw the stockings drying by the fire. If he could just throw the little packet of gold to land over by the fireplace, they'd surely see it in the morning, and it'd be safe from thieves. He just had to make sure he didn't throw it into the fire. All right, he used to play ball with his friends as a boy. He could do this. He bounced the bag of gold in his hand, feeling its weight. One – two – three! He tossed it in lightly.

He almost let out a bark of laughter! His aim was *too* good. He'd aimed at the longest stockings, knowing they were Rebekkah's. Her father would certainly know the gift was for her, no matter where it landed, but he had to aim at something. Well? The bag flew across the room and plopped right into the top of those stockings! He could even see the bulge at the toe. He had to clamp his hand across his mouth to keep from laughing. It was too perfect. Oh to be a fly on the wall here the next morning! He crept away, full of love and the giddiness of giving a gift that would bring magic and peace to someone. Such fun.

❧

The following morning, the girls awoke with sleepy smiles. Rebekkah had shared a tiny piece of the joy of her previous day with them all. It made the girls silly and giggly and her father smiled in genuine fondness for his oldest daughter. He'd been wracked with guilt and shame all night. His poor heart wanted more than anything to give Rebekkah the dowry she deserved, and he knew Stephen would be knocking at his door any day asking for her hand in marriage. Stephen had already hinted about it to him, but after the day the two of them shared yesterday, he was certain. He had a feeling there was much, much more that happened than just a walk in the woods. Rebekkah had changed somehow. Her face didn't have the same furrowed brow. And her shoulders were lighter, like she'd let go of something heavy.

After a few hours of sleepless anxiety, he lifted his heart to God the Father. He'd prayed many prayers of desperation. But this time, he was honest with the Lord about his own guilt, his fears, his deep desire to help his daughter start out on a life of her own. He didn't have any answers, but for the first time in ages, he fell asleep in peace.

The next morning, after he woke up and washed and clothed himself, he was holding one ragged end of a loaf of bread, trying to figure out how to break it into three pieces for his girls. He'd skip a meal again.

Rebekkah was over by the fire and grabbed her gray stockings and pulled them toward her. But they were heavy. There was something in the toe. "Oh my! I think there's a mouse in my stocking!"

The other two sisters started yelling, "Ewww!!!! Get it out-get it out!!!!" The youngest hopped up on a chair squealing with delight. Rebekkah laughed. Her father knew she wasn't afraid of mice. Rats, maybe. It had probably burrowed in, hopefully there wasn't too big a hole where he'd dug around. Her father was well aware that she only had the one pair of stockings. Rebekkah carefully took the toe and tipped the stocking upside down. Slowly the little mouse was nudged out. And *kerplunk*! Instead of a mouse, a small heavy bag of velvet hit the floor with a *chink*.

He knew that sound. He whipped around and all four of them looked at the little bag, a circle of them surrounding this small parcel of dark blue. "Oh my..." he whispered. He and Rebekkah shot each other a look of wonder and hope.

Then they all raced to the bag at once. He picked up the bag and poured out the contents. Onto the floor dropped several gold pieces. Rebekkah's hand flew up to her mouth, tears coursing down her cheeks with a huge smile beneath it all.

The sisters started dancing and singing, clasping their hands in a circle together. Such delight and cheer hadn't been known in that household for many years.

❧

Outside, several yards away, Stephen was standing, shifting his weight from one foot to another in indecision. He knew with all his heart what he wanted, but he still feared the unknown of supporting a wife and family. He was fully prepared to ask for Rebekkah's hand in marriage without a dowry, but he worried about her father's pride in not being able to furnish one. So he stood. And he worried.

He felt a hand on his shoulder.

"Bishop!" he cried. "What are you doing here?"

The Bishop grinned making Stephen wonder what he was up to. "Go to her, son. God will provide."

Stephen sucked in his breath. How did he know? Perhaps his love for Rebekkah had been more plainly seen than he thought. That was unsettling. More importantly though, hope soared. He quickly looked at their door. Could he? Should he? Now?

The Bishop said, "I'd go now." The man seemed oddly omniscient, thought Stephen.

✍

Bishop Nicholas quickly walked away, leaving Stephen standing there, gathering his courage. The Bishop walked around the next house as fast as he could without drawing attention to himself. Then he crept up to the window he'd stood at the night before. Inside, the sisters were dancing and singing, the father was openly weeping, and Rebekkah had never looked lovelier. Even with being a little too skinny and her hair not having been brushed or braided yet, Rebekkah was beautiful.

There was a knock at the door that stopped all the commotion and the Bishop smiled mischievously. The father walked to the door and opened it. Rebekkah was already blushing. All three girls tried their hardest to hear what was being whispered at the door between their father and someone. Then, their father opened the door wide and in stepped Stephen.

Instantly, everyone could feel the ties between Stephen and Rebekkah. Like invisible tendrils pulling them together.

He only had eyes for her. "Rebekkah," he said, walking toward her. He took her hands in his, making the little girls gasp in excitement. "Will you have me?"

Rebekkah was only capable of nodding. His hand reached out to her cheek as she whispered, "Yes." He slowly drew closer to her and gently kissed her lips.

The young girls started clapping and squealing with delight. The father wept even more. Stephen and Rebekkah began to laugh as the dancing and childish singing erupted even more fully. Their father was brought into the clamor and such joy, such love radiated throughout the shabby little room, making it seem brighter and nobler than the most regal of palaces.

Outside, the Bishop sighed in contentment. A huge smile plastered to his face, he wiped at the few tears that had fallen. It was even more wonderful than he expected. He walked away, full and happy.

CHAPTER 10

"Oh, Father, that is a wonderful story," I said, surreptitiously wiping at a pesky tear that had formed at the corner of my eye. "What happened with them?"

Father Espinoza smiled, enjoying the fact that I'd been as moved as he. "Well, Stephen and Rebekkah were married and began teaching together as far as I could find out. It was quite unusual to have a husband and a wife both be able to read, so I found a few things written about it. Then, when the other sisters came of age, overnight another little parcel of gold was found in their stockings. Three dowries for three daughters."

"So that Bishop was *The* St. Nick," I said.

"Yes. The Bishop eventually came to be known as Saint Nicholas. There are many documents claiming that he performed countless other miracles of generosity and incredible love for the unlovely. I like him. I think I like his pure enjoyment the most. Sometimes religious people are so boring. Don't you think?"

I chuckled. Yes, I did think that. "Oh you're not boring, though. I think you're probably as rascally as St. Nicholas," I said, making him laugh.

"I probably am," he said. "Well? I need to run. Please let me know if I can be of further assistance. I enjoyed our time very much. And be sure to keep me posted when your articles come out! I would very much love to read them."

We said our goodbyes, and once again I was thankful for having met another amazing person I could call a friend. What was the deal with this assignment? I sat down on a bench after I got a bottle of water from a vendor. I started pulling my thoughts together about the piece. I thought through the order of the stories and possible approaches to see if I could really tease out the magic of what I was feeling and make the readers feel it, too. I hoped my words would do it justice. But the best approach, I knew, would be to look at the root of the event. Every event of magnitude started with a person. With an idea. That's why these human interest stories were the crux of my article. They showed *why* something happened. I pulled out my laptop and started writing.

After about an hour that only felt like ten minutes – I was having so much fun – I received a text. Thank God it was from Drew. My patience with him was just about at its limits.

"Got what I needed. Meet up for dinner?"

"Sure. Where?"

"My place okay?"

You bet it was. "Yep!"

"Great. C U at 7."

"Perfect."

I ended up running back to my hotel so I could take a quick nap. I like naps. I treated them horribly as a child, and now I felt I should make it up to them. Besides, I was dog-tired. New York made me constantly tired and starving. I'm not sure if it's all the walking, all the people, or all the stimulating things bombarding you relentlessly. Probably all of the above. My feet and legs were so tired. And seriously, I was ravenous. I happily bought a hot dog from a vendor with all the fixings.

At 6:45, I was walking along 83rd on my way to see the cute guy and the amazing townhouse. I was dying to see what the place was like inside. The dark sky was a fabulous backdrop to all the buildings lit up and glittering. People were out en masse, the energy palpable and fun. I went for a more casual look tonight, with my favorite dark jeans and a dark green lightweight sweater with a deep V in the front. I came up to the white townhouse and it was even more charming at night. Most of the windows had lights shining out and it couldn't possibly look more welcoming. I paused and enjoyed the sight, remembering leaning up against the railing after Drew had slammed the door in my face. Good times.

I laughed to myself. The front door opened just then, and a warm light poured out. Drew stood at the top of the stairs in jeans and a gray Henley. He looked pretty delicious. "Are you coming in or are you worried I'll slam the door again?" he asked with a devilish smile. I laughed and started climbing the stairs.

"Oh, the night is young, but I'll take my chances, thanks."

Inside I could smell dinner and music was playing. The living room was ahead of us, with stairs going up and down to the left. It was decorated with masculine flair, but with a lot of personal artwork, pictures and books settled around. I loved when you walked into a place and got a real sense for the person who lived there. I hated walking into a place that was beautiful, but with just about as much personal oomph as walking into a Pottery Barn.

"Dinner's almost ready, do you want to come down to the kitchen while I finish up?" he asked as he was slipping off my coat. Right then my stomach growled, nice and loud.

"I'll take that as a yes."

"Good idea. I'm starving. As you can tell." He laughed.

"It's always nice to cook for someone who appreciates it." He ran down the spiral stairs and I followed him. The kitchen was at street level, so the windows peeked out at the sidewalk. There were thickly slatted shutters that let in light, but also gave a modicum of privacy. He had a bottle of wine set out with two glasses. It had already been opened. "Would you pour us a couple of glasses?"

"You got it," I said, as I started to pour.

He went over to the stove and started stirring pots. "So tell me about your day!"

I was dying to hear more about *his* day, but I truly was excited to share the two new stories I'd gotten. Plus the two more interesting people that told the tales. I thought of Poppy and her father, and how they both felt more complete when they shared their stories with each other. It was true. It's so satisfying. So I relayed the Fessenden story and Drew loved the bits about the 1906 earthquake. And then I told the story about the first Christmas stockings and Saint Nicholas. I didn't know if I was a good verbal storyteller, I focused so much on writing. But Drew was listening with rapt attention.

By this time, we were sitting at the cozy kitchen table, eating our stir-fry. It was delicious, hot and spicy and sweet. I ate everything. Two helpings.

Drew was sitting back from the table, his ankle comfortably crossed on his knee, contemplating the story with Stephen and Rebekkah. I sat back, sipping my Chardonnay and wondering what he was thinking about.

After a few more moments, he said, "You know? I never thought about it that way before. You always hear in church that Jesus came for the lost, the sinners, you know... But I think that's easy to overlook until you yourself do something even you can't excuse. And it's hard to accept forgiveness, I think."

"Yeah, I know what you mean," I said. "It's really powerful, right? I remember a time with my brother Jim. I had done something – I can't even remember now what it was – but I was in my early twenties and definitely knew better and I really hurt him. I ended up going to him to apologize, and I was just kicking myself for hurting him. I'd watched my mother and father for years; they'd hold grudges and keep tabs on who hurt whom so they could keep score. I figured Jim would lord it over me forever, you know?" Drew nodded. "But I went to him and apologized and I could see it written all over his face that he completely forgave me and was simply letting it go. Not once did he ever lord it over me, or remind me about it. And it was weird, we were even closer afterward."

"He sounds great," said Drew.

"He is. You'd like him. So how about you? Are you ready to tell me about what you ran off to do last night? You're killin' me here!"

He chuckled. "Yeah, I'm sorry about that. Our family has had to deal with a lot of issues because of that letter. It changed the course of events for many of us, and I'll tell you about all that later. I thought that part of the letter, the part you have, was lost forever. I'd kept our half but I couldn't remember which safe place I'd put it. It was something that I used to look at pretty frequently, but I had to be sure I still had it. I needed to put my hands on it." He was shaking his head in disbelief. His pretty, pretty head. "I just can't even tell you how crazy this is. I can't believe you have that letter!" He had an intense gleam in his eye. His enthusiasm was palpable.

"I brought it, let's go get it," I said. We went upstairs and I picked up my bag to retrieve the letter. I followed him into the living room and sat in the corner of a large, oatmeal colored sectional sofa. There were little lights everywhere, bookshelves on one of the walls, another wall was brick. It was beautiful and welcoming.

"So which 'safe place' was it? Where did you find your part of the letter?" I asked.

"Oh I'll never divulge my secret hiding place," he declared.

I looked around the room. Plenty of hiding places. In the corner, there was an old record player and a collection of jazz albums mixed in with The Stones, The Beatles and The

Doors. It was there; I just knew it. "You put it in one of your albums, didn't you?"

"Pffff. Whhhh," he blustered. "No. It wasn't there," he lied.

I rolled my eyes. I pulled out my half of the letter with a flourish. "Are you ready?" I asked.

He made a strangled sound, "Argh! Just give it to me, I'm dyin'!" His face looked so eager and strained, I laughed and relented.

So he held it, and I moved in next to him and read it over his shoulder. "No wonder you're dying to read the second half! What a cliff-hanger!" he exclaimed.

"So do you have the second half?" I asked. He nodded, his mental gears going full speed. He was holding his chin, tapping his mouth with a finger, thinking and considering. "Drew? Remember me? Sitting here? Dying?"

"Yeah, let me get the letter." He walked quickly over to the records, throwing me a disgusted yet sheepish look, and pulled the letter out of the John Coltrane, *Giant Steps* album. In his hand was the same sort of vellum. I took it and he settled in up against me, reading along with me. I darn well noticed his closeness; he smelled fantastic, but my curiosity about Willow's letter won over the moment.

I put the end of my letter up over the beginning of Drew's letter. The same handwriting, and from what I could tell, the same age and type of paper. It was most definitely a match. Where mine ended with the writer about to say farewell to the German, and the German handed him...

...a small book. It was diminutive like an address book and it clearly was dear to him. I started to say No, I couldn't take this. But he was adamant. I'd seen that look before. Men sometimes get a notion that they aren't going to make it. And many times, that particular look in the eyes is accurate. He was almost desperate that I take it. So I did. I clasped his hand in mine, hoping he'd see the agony in my eyes of not wanting to fight him in this damn war. I think he did. Marc smiled and let go. I never saw him again. This is the book he gave me. Keep it safe, Dearest. It means more to me than I can say. I love you, Willow. I feel more peaceful now that I can share this with you. Give the boys my love. I hope they won't forget me, they're so little. I'll have you in my heart always. My love, Herbert."

I sniffed. "Stupid letter," I said as I wiped away a tear.

Drew softly chuckled, "Herbert was a lover." He shook his head, "I just can't believe the letter is finally together. It seems so random, I can't fathom how this happened."

"It's quite a story, isn't it? But all these stories have a miraculous bent, don't you think? It still happens. Just when you think life is mundane, something incredible like this happens. I sure would like to have met that German soldier, Franz," I said.

"You mean Marc," said Drew.

"No, the letter says Franz," I said, clearly remembering Franz.

I looked at Drew who had a curious expression on his face. "Can I see the letters again?" he asked with a squeaky voice. I handed him the entire packet of papers.

He flipped through the papers, back and forth, checking and double-checking. A slow, secret smile formed on his face. The five o'clock shadow on his jaw was very nice to look at. His sleeves were pulled up over his forearms and I liked the look of his capable arms. And you just can't beat a soft gray shirt over good shoulder muscles.

He looked at me suddenly, a big grin on his face. "I have to go."

"Why do you keep doing that?"

CHAPTER 11

Men. Unbelievable. That night didn't end *at all* the way I wanted it to. He hadn't quite run out the door like he had the night before. But he also forgot the big kiss he'd at least planted on me before leaving. He'd shuffled me out the door, kissed my forehead, which *fine,* that was sorta' nice... And then Cinderella ran down the street. Again. I leaned up against the railing of the steps just like I had the first day I met him. I might have considered this rude behavior – running off and all – but even as I watched him speed-walk down the block, he had a skip in his step. And jeez, his smile was like a little kid's as he thought of whatever errand he so desperately needed to do... Well, call me a softy. How could I be mad at that?

At the very least, I had a good email waiting for me back at the hotel. Moxie, my editor's assistant, wrangled a call with a Civil War historian for later the following day. I had no idea why I needed that, but Moxie did and that was cool. I also had a very interesting voicemail. It was Father Espinoza inviting me back to the Chelsea seminary the next morning. He had a surprise.

ॐ

My phone buzzed. Then it buzzed again. Who is texting me? I looked at the clock through bleary eyes. Sheesh. It was only 6:30 in the morning. I pulled my phone toward me, squinting at the brightness of the screen, trying to read the text.

The first text said, "Morning!"

The second said, "Coco! Are you there?"

It was Drew. And he seemed chipper even through a text. I'm not fond of chipper morning people. But I couldn't help a small smile forming in spite of my grogginess. I was squinting to see the screen since I hadn't put in my contacts yet. I texted back what I hoped said, "Morning Cinderella. 6:30 too early. You're awfully chipper."

"Lol. Wanna meet at Grand Central for breakfast?" Now I was getting less grumpy.

"Sure. Make sure there's bacon. Are you going to stay the whole time this time?"

"??? Oh. Cinderella. Got it. Yes. I promise not to run out anymore. Unless you turn into a pumpkin, then I'm outta' there. I guarantee bacon."

"Perfect. Where should we meet? Can't meet before 8."

"8 is great. Go to the main hall in Grand Central, follow the signs. Let's meet under the clock. You can't miss it."

"I saw Madagascar. I remember the clock."

"☺ See you soon, Coco."

Well, now I was far less grumpy. I skipped over to the coffee maker, turned it on and jumped into the shower.

Just before 8 o'clock, I walked over toward Grand Central. There are about a hundred doors leading into the place. How do you know which one to go in? I tried the first one I came to and it opened into a big long hallway full of people. I started walking and sure enough, high up on the arches of the ceiling, were directions. I followed the signs to the main concourse, passing armed marines that I wanted to check out – who doesn't like a guy in uniform – but wasn't sure that they appreciated *appreciative* glances. I stole one anyway. One of them was a girl.

I walked into the cavernous hall and was instantly captivated. I *loved* this place. People were walking quickly every which way, the sea-foam-green ceiling soared above us all. It was painted with the constellations and tiny pinpoints of light sparkled like the stars they represented. It made me happy. It's just a building, but it simply made me smile and enjoy the moment. I ate up every detail of the ceiling and high windows, and finally looked around for the clock in the center of the room. Sure enough, right where Melman the giraffe gets his head stuck in a clock in the cartoon movie *Madagascar*, was a real-life brass clock. Beneath it was a very handsome man with his ankles casually crossed as he leaned on the wall supporting the clock, regarding me with a wide smile.

I returned that smile and walked over to him. "I love this place!" I exclaimed.

He looked around with me. "Yeah. It never gets old. I go out of my way just to be able to walk through here sometimes."

"I would, too," I said.

"See up there?" he said, pointing up to a far corner. "Look for a small blackish square, way up there."

"Yeah, I see that."

"That's from when they refurbished the building. The ceiling was *that* dark and they wanted to leave a small square so we'd remember what it used to be like."

"Wow. How'd it get so dark? Pollution?" I asked.

"That's what everyone thought, but when they tested it, it wasn't from the pollution of car exhaust, it was from cigarette smoke. All those years, millions of cigarettes being lit and smoked in here."

"Yikes."

"I know. Hey, let's walk around and since it's nice out, let's get a breakfast sandwich or pastry or something in Bryant Park."

"Great! As long as there's bacon, lead the way," I said.

We walked through the hall, up a long ramp and popped outside. We were walking along 42nd Street, going west toward Times Square. I was definitely starting to get the hang of this city.

Drew pointed out the main branch of the public library with the famous stone lions out front. Bryant Park was directly behind it. It was a beautiful day, suddenly warmer in the mid-60s. All I needed for a coat was a jean jacket. I wore a sleeveless dress, glad that I thought to bring a lot of layers. I was constantly too hot or too cold. I think that because you walk everywhere here, you build up a lot of energy. It could feel cool outside, then you briskly walk to the subway and suddenly you're too hot. Layers are key.

"You look smug," said Drew, laughing.

"Do I?" I laughed. "I was just thinking that I'm starting to get the hang of this place. I like that feeling."

"You should! People seem to either love New York City or hate it. And they don't mind telling you if they hate it."

"Well, that's annoying."

"Hah! It is. New Yorkers *are* arrogant about how great their city is, but we'd never pick on where someone else lives. Except New Jersey. We definitely pick on that. However, everyone who hates New York City will tell you blatantly even after you just told them you live there."

We walked into the park and Drew explained that they were prepping for the holiday bazaar, The Winter Village. "Usually, there's a big grassy space there in the middle," he said. "Right now they're getting it ready for the ice skating rink. It opens October 30th, so it's not quite ready yet." He pointed out where there'd be a big Christmas tree and about a hundred booths with crafts and food and other merchandise, surrounding the park.

We picked out a pastry, a big bacon and egg sandwich, and two cups of coffee at a stand at the west side of the park. "Let's sit over there," said Drew, directing us toward one of the many green metal tables and chairs dotting the whole area.

I bit into the steaming chocolate croissant.

"You look like a satisfied cat, Coco," said Drew.

"I am. Mmmm," I said happily. "This is delicious."

"Should I get you another one?"

"Yes."

I laughed as he quickly ran over to get me another croissant. See? Constantly ravenous.

He came back grinning as I had indeed finished my first one and was wiping off the crumbs from my face. And lap. I was hoping I hadn't gotten crumbs in my hair like Poppy most certainly would have.

"Thank you," I said.

"You are most welcome. Glad to be of service."

I filled him in on my upcoming appointments for the day as I enthusiastically moved on to the bacon and egg sandwich. I did share half of it with him. Reluctantly. Then I asked him, "So did you accomplish whatever it is that was so pressing last night?"

"I really am sorry I had to run out, Jane," he said, reaching out and covering my hand with his. "Did I make you mad?"

"No! Don't be silly. I couldn't be mad. You looked like a little kid who had to run home after school so he could see the new puppy his parents gave him." He looked grateful and laughed at my analogy.

"I felt like that. Can you wait for me to fill you in tonight? I have one more thing I want to get to show you first. Would you mind?" I did mind! I am not patient when it comes to fulfilling my curiosity. My face must have showed that because he said uncertainly, "Well… Maybe I could tell you now…"

"No, that's okay," I relented. "I can wait. I may not be patient, but I like a surprise that's properly complete. Do it right."

"Great. So is dinner okay? I can call you later with where to meet. Let me think about a good place."

"Sure! I have to get down toward Chelsea Piers again after this. I'm going to the Episcopal Seminary again to meet Father Espinoza. Should I take a cab from here?" I asked.

"Yeah, it'll be easier than walking or the subway. Actually, let me get you a car. There are a few car services that are even better than a cab."

He picked up his phone and started poking around. "Thanks. That'd be great. After that, I'm coming back up here for my video call." I motioned across the park toward the office where I was scheduled to have my meeting.

He saw me looking in that direction and said, "It's over there? You have to try Lady M Cake Boutique. The Mille Crepe cake is amazing."

"I can do that."

"Okay. Your car will pick you up on the northeast corner of 42nd and Sixth Avenue in about ten minutes. Let's go. I'll walk you over."

We stood up, threw out our trash and started to walk in that direction. We were walking closely, taking a few stolen moments to surreptitiously touch each other. I loved that tension: wanting to touch, but not ruining a moment by being too direct; stealing the chance to brush our hands against each other.

I know *my* heart was pounding, but I realized his was too when he suddenly said, "Oh forget this." He grabbed my hand and twisted me toward him so we were pressed up against each other, his arm circling around my back. "I didn't properly do this last night," he whispered, inches from my lips. He kissed me slowly, a fantastic knee-wobbling kiss.

"That's better," I whispered, with a smile.

"Definitely."

We walked hand-in-hand across the street to the right corner. He looked at his phone and said, "Yep! Right on time. Here's your car."

I walked to the back door of the car and he opened it for me. He said, "It's all paid for, and it will take you right to the seminary."

"Thanks! I'll call you after my meeting, okay?"

"Okay. See you soon."

I enjoyed looking around as we drove west and south. We arrived at the seminary right on time. I once again found Father Espinoza outside, bobbing up and down in eager anticipation. This time, with a twinkle in his eye, he led me to the library inside instead of taking a walk along the High

Line. We walked through many corridors and at last came to a library akin to what I've imagined from Disney's *Beauty and the Beast*. The walls and walls of books were killer. The room was at least two stories high, with spiral staircases here and there to get to the second level of books. Tables lined the floor of the great room, and sunlight entered from tall windows at one end.

I looked around, and seated at a long table smack in the middle of what was now my favorite room on earth, was... *Wonder Woman*. I'm not kidding. She was a tall, slender, buxom woman with a full and luxurious head of black hair. The only things missing were the cool golden cuffs and magic lasso. And she was an intimidating specimen of a woman, I might add. I was intimidated by the cartoon version; imagine the real life perfection.

Wonder Woman was studiously taking notes from a book the size of Kentucky. She looked up, her glossy black hair framing an intelligent face full of curiosity. I could easily imagine her in a college lecture hall bombarding her professor with question after question. I imagined her as someone constantly striving to know more, incessantly learning and applying.

Father Espinoza brought me over and introduced us. This was Lucy Langford, a seminary student. I shook her hand and joined her at the table as Father Espinoza quickly brought us a tray of coffee and ice water.

"Father Espinoza tells me he has a surprise. Are you part of the surprise, Lucy?" I asked.

I felt Father Espinoza silently chuckle as he sat down next to me. Lucy answered in a lovely deep voice, "Yes, I suppose I am. He filled me in on your article. As we got to talking yesterday afternoon, I realized I have a wonderful human interest story as to how Santa Claus came to be as we know him today."

"Oh that would be fantastic!" I said. "I've done a little research on him, and Father Espinoza gave me an excellent story on Saint Nicholas and how he is the one who is credited with surprise gifts overnight, especially to the needy, and also the idea of placing the gifts in stockings."

She nodded, taking her glasses off and clasping her graceful hands together in front of her on the table. "I know of that legend! I would love to hear more details of your story as well, Father."

"Of course," said Father Espinoza eagerly.

"What is your story about, Lucy?" I asked, taking out my laptop and phone, ready to record her story. Father Espinoza was fairly humming and buzzing with eagerness as I prepared. I looked at him. "You're not excited, are you?" I asked with a smirk and a cocked eyebrow.

"Oh yes, very. I am eager to hear Lucy's story in full," he said, completely missing my good-natured sarcasm. But she had caught it and bit back a smile at his earnest reply.

"All right. Well, do you know much about the Victorian images of Santa Claus?" she asked.

"No, not much more than the Saint Nicholas legends."

She started to inform us that the roots of Santa Claus can

indeed be traced back to Saint Nicholas of Bari, born in the 4th century in Lycia, currently a part of Turkey as Father Espinoza had explained. He was known to be wise, kind, prayerful, and incredibly generous. The date of Nicholas' death, December 6th, around the year 350 was one of such sadness, that the whole area of Asia Minor mourned and held a commemorative feast on December 6th, Saint Nicholas' Day. On Saint Nicholas Day Eve, kids would put out food for Saint Nicholas and straw for his donkey, and in the morning they'd find their gifts replaced with candies and toys.

Lucy brought out some pictures and laid them down one at a time. She was genuinely enthralled with this history and it was enjoyable to watch her enthusiasm.

"The gist is that throughout Europe, Saint Nicholas was reinvented in each country. In Germany Saint Nicholas became Weinachtsmann (Christmas Man), who worked as a helper to the Christ child and together they distributed gifts to children. In France, Pere Noël took root. He would bring special cakes, cookies and candies and always left the goodies in the children's shoes. In Russia, Father Frost came about – he distributed gifts in January when the Russian church observed Christmas. And in England, Father Christmas was a tall, thin, elderly man who had a long beard and carried a large sack of toys."

The last picture looked a lot like Gandalf.

"Looks like Gandalf," muttered Father Espinoza. I almost spit out my mouthful of coffee and Lucy cracked a smile.

The odd thing to me, that I hadn't known was that these early forbears of Santa started to collect some "helpers." The two most popular were Knecht Ruprecht and Belsnickle

– but they were both totally scary! Carrying rods and switches. Together with Santa, they would reward *and* punish, definitely representing the lovely relationship children had with their parents during this era… which is why Lucy was telling us all this. Santa had had a big makeover somewhere along the way. She even brought out a few pictures of these helpers.

"Are you kidding?" I exclaimed. "Coal black little devil guy with horns?" She nodded. "Talk about your nightmare." Father Espinoza crossed himself and I blurted out, "I didn't think Episcopalians crossed themselves."

"Sure we do. Here, I'll do it for you, too." He crossed himself again, shuddering at the demon images of Santa's helpers. A serious departure from *Elf* and *The Polar Express*.

As Lucy took a drink of water, I had an opportunity to ask a quick question. "So Santa had a makeover at some point, to become what we know of him today: jolly, happy, generous… I'd also read somewhere that Christmas itself, the way the holiday was celebrated, wasn't always what we know today, either."

Lucy nodded enthusiastically. "That's true. The holiday coincided with Winter Solstice and it was more like Mardi Gras. It was raucous, unwholesome and certainly not for children in the 1600's. Groups of drunk people would mill around looking for trouble and crime would escalate at that time. So, when the Puritans came to America in 1620, they made it illegal to even mention Saint Nicholas's name. People also couldn't sing carols, exchange gifts or anything."

"Hah! People always say the old days were kinder and gentler. Not so much," I remarked.

Lucy laughed, "Certainly not. More than 150 years passed before any mention of St. Nick first appeared in some American newspapers, probably due to German or Dutch influences but some papers in 1770s called him Saint A. Claus and wrote about his generosity.

"It's perfect that you came to New York to research this, Jane," she continued. "There are two important New York City links to the popularity of Christmas in general, and Santa specifically. The first is this: in the early 1800s, the New York Historical Society recognized Saint Nicholas as its patron saint, going back to the city's Dutch roots.

"Children found it very tantalizing that some other children were getting gifts from *Sinterklaas* which became *Santy Claus* and eventually *Santa Claus*."

"I bet!" I said, as I nodded.

She continued, "In 1808 Washington Irving wrote about Sinter Klaas in his book *A History of New York*. He describes the visitor as a fat little man in a typical Dutch Costume, with knee britches and a broad-brimmed hat, who traveled on a flying horse-drawn wagon dropping gifts down the chimneys on the Eve of Saint Nicholas Day, December 6th. And the familiar phrase, 'Laying his finger beside his nose' first appeared in Irving's story, too.

"Next comes the second New York City link. And that is where my story picks up. It took a professor of theology to really give Santa the form that we are used to. And he's a key factor in Santa's visit coming on December the 24th, Christmas Eve, instead of St. Nicholas' Day, December 6th, or Epiphany, on January 6th."

"Okay! Lay it on us!" I said, full of all the Christmas history I'd known nothing about.

Lucy sat back in her chair, took a deep breath and let a

satisfied sigh escape her lips. "It started with an average woman, leading an average life, who would soon be the impetus that changed the world…"

CHAPTER 12

Chelsea, New York City
December 1822

"No, no, no. You cannot continue that line of thinking, Clement Clarke Moore!" His aunt's brusque manner made him smile. She was so earnest in her beliefs, but it was all just silliness. She went on, "Your mother and I have been friends since before you were born. Oh! And darn these skirts, excuse my language dear, but they keep getting in my way!" They were walking down the street just getting some fresh air, but Josephine was so intent on her persuasive efforts, that she was walking at a good clip and her long skirts were just not moving as quickly as she was.

"Aunt Barton, do be careful. Don't trip and hurt yourself," he said, holding out his arm for his aunt to hold.

She did take his arm, but she wasn't pleased. "Honestly, Clement, you were such a daring young child, but these days you are so somber. So serious. And your views of Christmas are quite unreasonable. Your children are more concerned with their studies than that blessed day, and they are so young, dear. Children should be playing and enjoying some merriment around the day they celebrate Christ's birth.

"Clement," she continued, "I will never get over missing my children. They grow into adults so quickly. But when you're in the middle of those years, they don't feel so fast. But they are. I just… I want you to remember the magic of childhood."

"Oh, but Aunt Barton, that's just foolishness," he said. "Look here; I am working on developing this area of

Chelsea for the city. Today it's countryside, but soon it will be a thriving village and hopefully a seminary. There are such important things going on, how could I possibly work on helping the children to… oh, *experience* the holiday? It seems a waste of time. They have their own imagination, that's good enough. They don't need me to help with that."

She glanced at his high collar, analyzing his face, even the curls on top of his head, making him self-conscious.

She looked like she'd come to some sort of decision. "Clement. I ask you, do this one thing. Do you promise?"

He gave her a rather put-out look and said, "Well I can't promise if I don't know what it is."

"You are such a stubborn man," she muttered. "Do you remember how you used to climb the pine trees?"

Surprisingly, a small grin appeared on his face. He nodded. "And do you remember how it would foster long talks and deep questions?"

Indeed he did. For some reason the energy put forth, the expansive view, the spicy scent of pine… It all came together to give him an unusual perspective. Therefore it filled him with profound questions and deep thoughts. His favorite person to share this with had been Aunt Barton.

"I do. I clearly remember it," he said, fully happy to have satisfied her question.

"You need to go climb the tree again."

"Wh- Wh," he sputtered. "That's outrageous. A grown man mustn't climb trees. Preposterous."

"Oh stop blustering. Just think about it. If it did you such good back in those days, what's it really harming now?" Then she muttered, "…and it wouldn't hurt for your children to see you enjoy yourself for once."

"What was that?" he asked, reasonably certain he'd

160

heard her properly.

"Oh… Just go climb the tree. Then give it some thought about what I said about Christmas and your children." She stomped off in a huff, her wide hat bouncing up and down, making him chuckle. She sounded abrupt, but her demeanor was so sincere, so adorable, he could never be offended with her. He had quite a soft spot for his aunt.

Clement was a little unsure of what this was all about. She'd been hinting around at something about Christmas for a month at least. But he just couldn't understand the fuss she was making. As the day progressed, he worked at his typical daily duties. He worked on his accounting tasks, he saw his wife about some household details for the party coming up, he spoke with some of his carpenters who'd been helping with a variety of projects on the estate, and then it was time for dinner.

He'd barely seen the children that day. There were nine of them, so of course they were a busy household and the nannies would give them dinner early and whatnot. He wondered what they'd been up to all day. He loved his children. The oldest were getting so interesting, and the little ones were such dear things. Maybe he'd run upstairs and see what they were up to before he and his wife had their dinner.

But as he bounded up the stairs, he realized the little ones were in bed already. He'd been outside and missed their "goodnights." Perhaps the older ones were still awake. He peeked his head into the study. His two eldest children were there, working on their homework.

"Benjamin. Mary. How are you?" he asked.

Benjamin didn't look up, but said cheerily enough, "Fine, thanks, Father. How are you?"

Mary asked, "How was work today?"

"I was very productive," he said.

She looked back at her own work as she smiled, "I'm glad."

They sure were working hard on the day before Christmas Eve. Hmm. Perhaps Aunt Barton had a point. He'd figured the children would enjoy the magic of the holidays enough on their own. He always had. But then again, his father loved presents even more than his own children. Not a selfish bone in his body, he was still tickled pink when he received a present. Every time, he'd do this little jig with his elbows flapping up and down. Eventually they called it the Present Dance. He laughed a little at this thought, making Benjamin and Mary look up at him.

"Are you all right, Father?" asked Benjamin.

Oh good heavens. These children of his were going to need a lesson in having fun.

"Put away your books," said Clement.

Mary had a quizzical look on her face as if he'd just spoken Mandarin. He rubbed his forehead. "Um… I have a project for you both. Get your outdoor clothes on and meet me out back. Right away." They both liked projects.

"But it's started to snow!" Benjamin objected.

"So wear your warmer clothes. On the double! Let's go!"

Clement fairly ran to his room to change. Now that the idea of going out in the snow so late at night was taking shape, he was a little giddy about it. Oh! Dinner! He plum forgot. He still changed into his outdoor casual clothing instead of his finer dinner jacket that he'd typically wear; Catherine would understand. Knowing her, she'd probably join in…

He raced down the stairs, told Catherine his plan, and ran out the door. A couple of the servants looked at him in wonder and not a little consternation.

After happily clumping around in the snow a bit, he finally heard the door slam shut and saw Ben and Mary coming outside. Mary still had the shorter skirts of younger girls and a good thing, too. Long skirts make it hard to climb a tree.

"Climb a tree?" both Mary and Ben shouted at the same time after he had explained his plan.

Ben argued, "We barely climb trees in the summer now, let alone in December!"

"Well perhaps you should," said Clement simply. "Suit yourself." At that, he started walking over to the pine tree he had his eye on. It wasn't as easy to see out of the full branches of an evergreen, as compared to a bare maple tree, but you could climb so high on the many sets of branches, and he truly wanted to smell that scent that captivated his imagination. "You two should try the maple!" It was right next to the tall fir tree.

He crept under the lowest branches of the 40-foot pine, the branches nearest the ground having been trimmed. He gripped the branch at chest level, located a man-sized path to head up toward, and started climbing. He watched his children debating about what to do and how to tackle this problem of climbing. He smiled to himself. He knew they couldn't be out-done by their old father. Sure enough, they started climbing the maple. Ben first, followed closely by Mary. All three of them found a good, firm branch to sit upon.

The snow was still falling, but lightly. It wasn't the thick sort of snow that you could hear falling, but it did muffle the sounds of the night. It was so bright out, and the moon was full. His house looked beautiful, glistening in the light.

"Are you looking forward to Christmas?" he asked, watching Mary kick her legs in the air as she looked around.

"Oh, I suppose so, Father," said Benjamin. Did *he* sound this supercilious? Maybe he did. Maybe that was why Aunt Barton looked like she wanted to shake him.

"What, do you think celebrating Christmas is beneath you?"

Mary said, "It's not beneath me! But I do wish..."

"What, Mary? What do you wish?" he asked, since she paused.

"Well... I love that we have a Christmas tree and decorations. But my friends at school talk a lot about Father Christmas and the best stories are about Santy Claus." Clement liked those stories, too.

Ben burst in, "But those drawings of him! I don't think he looks all that kind."

"Yes," said Mary, "and his helper is scary. I don't like the thought of *him* coming into our home. But I do love the idea of surprises! Isn't there a good story of Saint Nicholas?"

"There is," said Clement. He told them about the saint who gave so much of his own money to the needy and figured out surprising methods of delivery.

"But I wonder how Santy Claus would get around so quickly to all the children? Do you think he'd come to our house, like our friends, through the front door?" asked Benjamin, sounding wonderfully sincere and more than a tad optimistic.

"That's a fine question, son. How would he get around? And how would he get into the homes without anyone knowing?"

"Oh I have that figured out," declared Mary. "He's magical anyway, but he goes down the chimney! It's the only way, with all the doors locked and all. Besides, the presents are always near the fireplace, so it makes sense."

"Except the bit about the *fire*," said Benjamin sarcastically.

"I *said* he was magical…" explained Mary, as if talking to a three-year-old.

"But do you really think he looks like the drawings, Papa?" asked Mary, forgetting she'd started calling him Father like Benjamin. It warmed his heart.

"Well, what do you think he looks like?" he asked them.

"Certainly not grim or angry," said Ben.

"And he should be a bit sweet and nice for children to be around. Someone they'd laugh with a lot," added Mary.

"Yes," said Clement, adding his own two cents, "and jolly. I'm still wondering about his conveyance, though. It would have to be extremely special. Something certainly magical as you said, Mary." She nodded importantly.

They all sat in their trees, looking around, enjoying a companionable silence.

"I like it up here," said Ben. "I should do this more often. I feel… better. And I didn't even know I'd been feeling *not* better." He had a self-deprecating grin that Clement could even see in the semi-darkness.

Clement felt better, too. Aunt Barton was right. Sometimes you need a new perspective. And it gave him a marvelous idea.

The next day dawned a lovely white and crisp Christmas Eve. The whole family was coming over and the house would be even fuller than the typical eleven family members. They'd feast on roast beef, mashed potatoes, cranberries, and more desserts than you could possibly even taste one single bite of!

After much eating, drinking, games, and merry-making, all of the cousins and aunts and uncles and grandparents settled down in the large living room. The fireplace burned brightly as did the Christmas tree with its little candles carefully hung here and there. Everyone was satisfied, replete, and the beginnings of yawns began to spread around the room. Before the little ones went to bed, Clement made an announcement.

"Everyone," he began, as he stood up in front of the massive tree, "thank you so much for making our Christmas a delightful evening. I have a little surprise for all of you. Especially for Aunt Barton. I want to thank you for your… exhilarating walk the other day." He winked at her as she smiled prettily at him.

Behind him on a little table, was a cranberry-red box. He took off the lid and pulled out a scroll. "I have a little poem I've written for this special and most generous of days. I was reminded this week that sometimes we need a new perspective, and that the days go by very quickly indeed. If we don't celebrate when we can, we will miss out on those precious hours. I hope that this little story will bring that kind of refreshment to you all."

He looked carefully at all nine of his children. Every one of them completely unique from the next; holding dreams in their hearts, unwritten plans for their futures still to be determined, hopefulness in each one of their sweet eyes. His own gratefulness at that moment almost overwhelmed him. And he was even more excited that he could offer them this poem.

He quietly cleared his throat, and began reading.

A Visit from St. Nicholas

'Twas the night before Christmas,
When all through the house
Not a creature was stirring, not even a mouse;
The stockings were hung by the chimney with care,
In hopes that St. Nicholas soon would be there;

He heard a small collective gasp from Benjamin and Mary, and smiled to himself. The littlest children, cousins and siblings, all got off their mothers' laps and inched forward, getting closer to him, now that they knew that this story was going to be *good*.

The children were nestled all snug in their beds,
While visions of sugar-plums danced in their heads;
And mamma in her 'kerchief and I in my cap,
Had just settled our brains for a long winter's nap.
When out on the lawn there arose such a clatter,
I sprang from my bed to see what was the matter.

Everyone gasped at this point, and his smallest daughter Catherine clapped her hands.

Away to the window I flew like a flash,

Tore open the shutters and threw up the sash.
The moon on the breast of the new-fallen snow,
Gave the lustre of mid-day to objects below.

Benjamin and Mary exchanged knowing glances and he almost teared up when Mary reached out to hold Benjamin's hand.

When, what to my wondering eyes did appear,
But a miniature sleigh, and eight tiny reindeer,
With a little old driver, so lively and quick,
I knew in a moment it must be St. Nick.
More rapid than eagles his coursers they came,
And he whistled, and shouted, and called them by name;

Adding a little dramatic gusto, Clement jumped up onto a nearby by ottoman and nicely bellowed,

"Now Dasher! Now, Dancer! Now, Prancer and Vixen!
On, Comet! On, Cupid! On, Donder and Blitzen!
To the top of the porch! To the top of the wall!
Now dash away! Dash away! Dash away all!"

He jumped back down and altered his voice to a lilting cadence. All the eyes in the room were fastened on him, wide with wonder, and imagining the vivid scene.

As dry leaves that before the hurricane fly,
When they meet with an obstacle, mount to the sky;
So up to the house-top the coursers they flew,
With the sleigh full of toys, and St. Nicholas too.

Three of the little boys spontaneously cheered at the mention of toys. He almost cracked up. Now the fun part. He moderated his voice to a mysterious whisper.

> *And then, in a twinkling, I heard on the roof*
> *The prancing and pawing of each little hoof.*
> *As I drew in my head and was turning around,*
> *Down the chimney St. Nicholas came with a bound.*
> *He was dressed all in fur, from his head to his foot,*
> *And his clothes were all tarnished with ashes and soot;*
> *A bundle of toys he had flung on his back,*
> *And he looked like a peddler just opening his pack.*
> *His eyes – how they twinkled! His dimples how merry!*
> *His cheeks were like roses, his nose like a cherry!*
> *His droll little mouth was drawn up like a bow*
> *And the beard of his chin was as white as the snow;*

Mary could hardly help herself and sighed contentedly at this wonderful image. Clement heard her murmur, "Dimples!"

> *The stump of a pipe he held tight in his teeth,*
> *And the smoke it encircled his head like a wreath;*
> *He had a broad face and a little round belly,*
> *That shook when he laughed, like a bowlful of jelly.*
> *He was chubby and plump, a right jolly old elf,*
> *And I laughed when I saw him, in spite of myself;*
> *A wink of his eye and a twist of head,*
> *Soon gave me to know I had nothing to dread;*
> *He spoke not a word, but went straight to his work,*
> *And filled all the stockings; then turned with a jerk,*
> *And laying a finger aside of his nose,*

And giving a nod, up the chimney he rose;
He sprang to his sleigh, to his team gave a whistle,
And away they all flew like the down of a thistle,
But I heard him exclaim, ere he drove out of sight,
"Happy Christmas to all, and to all a good-night!"

The children – and Aunt Barton – all at once leapt into the air, cheering and clapping! The older fellas hooted and hollered, the grandmas dabbed a tear, the women all hugged each other. And his wife Catherine came over to him, her face shining.

"Darling, that was the most wonderful Christmas present you could have ever given us all." And like the rascal she was, planted a big kiss right on his lips, eliciting "Eww!" from the boys and "Awww!" from the girls.

❧

Mrs. Barton reveled in the wonderful emotions flooding the room. She had no idea what Clement would do when she had talked with him; she just knew her talented nephew was in need of a little push. A little push to open his eyes and *see*. She had no idea he was capable of the potent gift he just gave their family. A gift of wonder, mystery and generosity. What a wonderful way to be reminded of God's lavish generosity, creativity and utter joy! She knew she needed to get that poem to more people.

Over the next few months, Clement told her he just wanted to keep the poem in the family. She wondered if he was embarrassed that he wrote a children's poem. She was certain he didn't understand what imagination it sparked in those who read it. And it contradicted those rather scary

170

portrayals of Santy Claus going around. So she came up with a plan.

The following November, she copied the poem without Clement knowing. And boy, did he have a surprise waiting for him that Christmas. But even she didn't realize how it would change people's lives forever. In the morning edition of the December 23rd, 1823, Troy New York Sentinel, *A Visit from St. Nicholas* by Clement Clarke Moore was published.

Christmas finally regained the enchanting imaginative color that it originally had, back in the day when angels appeared and real magic shook the earth.

CHAPTER 13

I had to suppress my own urge to jump up and cheer at the end of Lucy's rendition of *'Twas the Night Before Christmas*, as it came to be known. "So were there illustrations? How did this new image of Santa catch on?" I asked.

Lucy pulled her hair behind one ear and replied, "Well, the poem became famous and instantly made Santa an American Christmas institution. But there was still some debate as to what Santa really looked like. 40 years later, in 1863, Thomas Nast was a famous illustrator and caricaturist who created the donkey and elephant images for the Democratic and Republican parties. He was asked to illustrate *'Twas the Night Before Christmas*. He imagined the wording from Moore and gave the world a far less stern-looking Santa who was kind, gentle, and jolly. It's really the image you see all over the place."

She took out some illustrations to show us and, sure enough, I even recognized Nast's original drawing. Suddenly, something she said hit me. "Ooh. 1863, huh? So did Santa make an appearance at the Civil War? We were in the thick of it then."

Lucy turned a bright eye on me like a teacher who's surprised by an excellent comment from a mediocre student. I was pleased and annoyed at the same time.

"Good, Jane!" Shut up, Wonder Woman. I held back the urge to pant and bring her a toy so I could get a pat on the head. "Yes, Abraham Lincoln was so impressed with this new Santa, he asked Nast to draw the elf visiting with the Union troops around a battlefield campfire on Christmas

Eve. Supposedly this had a great impact on morale for the troops in the North. In each of Harper's December issues, Nast added to the legend of Santa Claus who was filling stockings. He's the one who came up with Santa's workshop and created the Naughty and Nice lists. Then in 1931, Santa got a final makeover. Artist Haddon Sundblom made billboards, magazine ads, and in-store displays for Coca-Cola. Sundblom's Santa replaced Nast's that was a tad harsher and not quite as smoothly drawn."

Father Espinoza and I thanked Lucy for her time, which I really did appreciate. But then I remembered one more question, "Hey, Lucy, how did you find out about this personal story of Clement Clarke Moore?"

She smiled, genuinely; she must've had a soft spot for her connection. "One of my ancestors was their maid. She heard the story that first night he read it in 1822; the servants had all come into the room, as well as the family, to listen to his surprise. It was a special night for her. She was only a teenager, but it stuck with her for her whole life. She told the story to her children and her grandchildren hundreds of times. And now I'm passing it on."

She looked like a satisfied cat. It made me think of how Mrs. Barton must have felt when she was able to get the original poem published for the world to enjoy. We finished our goodbyes and I promised to send her links to the articles when they came out.

As we left the seminary, I thanked Father Espinoza again and he gave me a bear hug. He was truly enjoying himself with this Christmas project. I marveled at the fact that these stories were taking me around the world so-to-speak, and I was meeting people from every walk of life. I also thought it was providence that the Civil War ended this conversation and would begin the next.

I had rented a WeWork space for the day so I could have my Google Hangout call and then work on my articles. If I went to my hotel, I'd want to nap. I decided to just walk back over to Bryant Park, so I had time to collect my thoughts. I walked forever, but eventually came to Times Square. I even peeked in at the giant Ferris wheel in the Toys R Us at 44th Street. I was a little disturbed at all the people dressed up like mascots walking along Broadway trying to get you to have your picture taken with them, for money of course. Elmo was particularly grungy.

I kept walking east and easily found Bryant Park. Having worked up an appetite, I located that Lady M Boutique bakery Drew told me about. Remember what I said about not liking desserts? I have a few exceptions. Like bread pudding and now the mille crepes at Lady M. I could eat a lot of those. Their vanilla cream mille crepes and a big cup of coffee hit the spot. Afterward, I went upstairs to the conference room I'd booked.

I walked up an incredibly colorful winding staircase. The railings were white with lacy cutouts on the wood railings and a bright mural ran along the walls. In fact, the colors and shapes gave me a funny feeling of déjà vous. It looked a little like Kandinsky. But that wasn't it. I'd have to chew on that for a while. I wondered why it seemed so familiar or like it had jogged a memory...

I got another coffee at the counter, then set up my laptop for my meeting in my reserved conference room. About ten minutes before my appointment, my phone rang.

"Hey there, Drew. How are you?"

"I'm good! Hey, do you feel like a steak tonight?"

"I do. I do feel like a steak." Yessir.

"Great! Let's go to Keens. 72 West 36th. Wanna' say seven?"

"I think that sounds like a plan," I chuckled. "See you later."

"Bye, Coco," he said, with a deeper, huskier voice, reminding me of that last kiss in Bryant Park. Ooh. Room swerve. I do like his voice.

Right at that very moment came the Google Hangout call. Perfect. Right when I was very befuddled. I couldn't find the right buttons and almost swept my coffee cup over. Good grief.

"Hi!" I exclaimed a little too brightly.

The man on the other end, a burly man in his 60s with short brown hair and a nice mustache, sort of popped back in his seat as if I'd frightened him. "Sorry, I uh... had some glitching and wasn't sure you could hear me," I lied. "How are you? I'm Coco, I mean, actually, Jane Smith." Smooth.

His dark brown eyes glittered with humor. "Hello, I'm Bruce Mueller." His mustache was just like Tom Selleck's. And it nicely accentuated his intelligent face. His dignified hands were clasped in front of him belying an impish grin. Hmm... I'd have to be on my toes with this one. Something about this Christmas topic was bringing all sorts of children-in-adult-clothing to the surface. No wonder I was having so much fun.

I quickly explained the gist of my project. I also highlighted the other sorts of stories I had received and how they lent a wonderful human interest aspect to bare historical facts.

Bruce filled me in about his background in Civil War history. At first it had been a hobby and personal passion. Then it consumed his imagination so much, he got his masters in history. I smiled at him, admiring his passion.

"Ooh! Have you ever participated in any reenactments?" I asked.

He got a funny look on his face. "Yes, and I assure you, reenactments are extremely helpful in understanding history," he said.

"I agree," I replied simply. "In fact, I write a lot of historical pieces on a specific moment in time. So I try to understand the complex emotions and values that you can easily dismiss when you're looking back from the future. I completely understand the desire to try to get yourself in a situation where you really *feel* a small taste of what it was like. I would love to participate in one."

He looked like he'd been ready for battle and didn't I just deflate all the arguments he had ready to go. He looked so quizzical, I laughed. "Caught ya' off guard, huh?"

"Well... Yeah." Then I swear he chuckled just like Tom Selleck. I was suddenly at the Sunday dinner table with Tom and his family in the TV show *Blue Bloods*.

"Anyway," I said, "I heard that the image of Santa by Thomas Nast really spoke to President Lincoln. Can you enlighten me on any other interesting tidbits?"

He grinned like a starving man served a big steak. He dug right in.

"Well. Let me give you a little context. At the end of the Civil War, when on Sunday, April 8th, 1865, Generals Grant and Lee met at Appomattox Courthouse and declared the war ended, about 360,000 Union and 260,000 Confederate soldiers had given their lives, roughly 2% of the population. In today's numbers, it would have equaled around 6 million people. America lost more people in the Civil War than in World War I, World War II, Vietnam, and the Korean wars combined. Disease played a large part. For every three deaths in combat, five more would occur from disease. Another destructive aspect for the country was that recruitment came from local areas, so people would go to war with their neighbors and cousins. When a regiment had major losses, it meant whole communities would be practically destroyed. Those years were bitter, hard-fought and heart-breaking.

"Abraham Lincoln was beyond what words can describe. He was a man of greatness. His wisdom, compassion and deep grief over the country's profound losses, yet inexpressible hope that we would overcome, was something rarely seen in human history. Since you're featuring the backstories about Christmas traditions, I wanted to share with you a story. One that ties two men and two perspectives together. And has a surprising link with Christmas. They were both deeply touched by Abraham Lincoln. I think through this account, you'll get a deeper feel for just what Lincoln meant to real people, far more so than just trying to describe him."

CHAPTER 14

New York City
Saturday, April 15th, 1865

The sun was shining and for the first time in years, the air carried the promise of hope of reconstructing our poor country from the ashes of war, death, and disease. He noticed that people had a look of lightness on their faces and felt freedom as they walked to synagogue, on that fine morning of the Passover week.

Oh, he would never forget that very first morning of Passover, the news! Oh the news! News of the meeting of the Generals at Appomattox Courthouse where the war officially came to an end. What timing! What a cosmic dance of perfection that this Festival of Freedom honoring the Israelite Exodus from centuries of slavery, should align with the end of American slavery. The Seder tables had been a mystic experience for him and his family as the words spoken every year, the words of the Haggadah, "Why is this night different from all other nights?" meant something profound both to ancient times *and* their time. Their culture. Their lives.

Joshua walked to temple with his neighbors, his friends and family. He'd graduated from Harvard just a few years ago and was working hard at becoming the lawyer his family hoped he'd be. Talk about hard won victories! Oh, the joy of new beginnings.

Joshua looked around him when he got to the corner of West 70th and Columbus. Something caught his eye at the corner fruit and news stand. A sudden movement. The rush of a few more people. There was something uncertain and furtive in the air. Growing more wary as the moments passed and the tension increased, he crossed the street to find out what was going on.

His friend, an old neighbor who'd lived in his building for as long as he could remember was standing there, her arms at her sides, her face white and her lip quivering. "Mrs. Goldberg! What is it? Are you all right? How can I help you?" he asked, touching her elbow to steady her.

"He's dead," she whispered, tears starting to fall from her watery dark eyes.

"Who?" he asked. He dreaded what could possibly have this effect on her.

"The President. Mr. Lincoln."

He gasped. All the sweet joy and peace was suddenly, horribly sucked out of him. "No."

Word was spreading. So was the awful reality. The man who had sacrificed so much, who had fought so hard, who had aged decades in his few years in office... had been assassinated.

A strange quiet affected the streets that day. More and more people came out onto the avenues, word quickly reaching the masses. Those who had been on their way to the Passover services, walked along half-aware, caught up in their own misery. Those who hadn't been planning on going, came out, too. Walking together, their own spontaneous walk of memorial toward the place where they could comfort, be comforted, and just be together.

His father and mother caught up to him. Their faces told him they'd heard the news. There were no words. His tall father put his hand out and rested it on Joshua's shoulder. It said enough.

They arrived at their beloved synagogue, the oldest in

America, and wearily went up the steps. One. Two. Three. His footsteps were weighted with profound shock and sadness. Inside, there were hushed whispers, occasional half-contained sobs, and the sounds of sniffles into handkerchiefs. It was not what they'd expected to be experiencing this day. This Passover.

As the rabbi came forward, his head was lowered, and his steps were slow and painful-looking. The congregation grew perfectly still. Waiting. What would he say? What *could* he say?

He looked out at his people, his eyes searching for the words that wouldn't come. He'd brought his sermon notes with him, and he put them aside. He began saying something about their heartbreaking loss, but was overcome and had to stop, his hand coming to his mouth and his head shaking slowly back and forth. Then he did the only thing he thought appropriate and right. The thing that would be controversial for many, but perfectly right for them, at that moment in time. He recited the Hashkabah.

The words of the prayers for the dead – the first time they were prayed in the oldest synagogue in America for a man not of Jewish lineage – rang through the air and into their hearts. At first haltingly, as the rabbi struggled with his own grief, then growing in joy, love and strength. "...May the destined soul of Abraham Lincoln be true repose under the wings of the Divine Presence in the celestial realm, the Chamber of the holy and pure shining resplendent as the luminous firmament... May the supreme Ruler of all earthly kings in mercy show this soul love and compassion. May peace attend him and his repose be peaceful as it is written: 'They shall enter into peace, they who walk in their uprightness shall have repose in their resting places.' May he and all his ancestors slumbering in the dust along with the other dead of Israel, be included in mercy and forgiveness. May this be the Divine Will, and let us say: AMEYN!"

At home later that day, Joshua's thoughts went to a friend of his from Harvard. The large, 6-foot 4-inch, 300-pound-man, with the heart of a child and the orator's skill of Lincoln himself, Phillips Brooks. After they'd graduated, the friends stayed in touch by letter. Joshua found himself inexplicably pulled to go to see him. It would take just as long to make the journey himself as it would to post a letter. So he boarded a train the very next day and headed to Philadelphia.

Joshua pondered this journey on his train ride. He knew beyond a doubt that he was supposed to go to his friend. Brooks had grown in fame as a powerful orator as he led the church of the Holy Trinity. His poet's heart worked wonders from the pulpit. Joshua smiled to himself as he remembered Phillips' vast knowledge of hymns. He'd told Joshua that it had been their family tradition for the children to memorize at least one hymn per week then recite it on Sunday evening. He carried a little book with him, with all those hymns written in it, some 212 hymns! He still knew them by rote.

Phillips loved children and acted like one himself when he was around them. Kids adored the big fella. He and his music director had begun a Sunday school program for children, in fact. It had started with 30 children. Within two years, over 1,000 children were attending each week.

But Joshua noticed Phillips' playful heart diminishing through the years of the War. His letters had grown increasingly downhearted as those long, bloody years dragged on. There was hardly a household that hadn't known death and suffering. It was hard indeed to shepherd such wide spread sorrow. Joshua thought that was why, perhaps, he felt this summoning to be with him. This final blow might be too hard. Too much injury in the midst of a rawness that hadn't been healed. And Phillips most definitely would be asked to orate at Lincoln's funeral. How could he endure it?

But he did endure, and on Sunday, April 23rd, Phillips gave a sermon at Lincoln's funeral that had to go down in history. Joshua would never forget the words of that eulogy, "In him was vindicated the greatness of real goodness, and the goodness of real greatness. The twain were one flesh. Not one of all the multitudes who stood and looked up to him for direction with such a loving and implicit trust and tell you today whether the wise judgments that he gave came most from a strong head or a sound heart."

The night following the funeral, the two friends took a long walk around the city and landed in a small English pub. The fire in the hearth made the place cheery, sending dancing shadows around the wood floors, high-backed leather booths and large mugs full of frothy ale. The city had begun the long journey of moving on after great mourning. Little glimpses of simple, normal life gave hope and small smiles to the beleaguered pub-goers. Joshua thought that might be why the place appealed to Phillips.

"Friend," said Joshua to Phillips, "You look as if you've been trying to figure something out. Have you done it yet?"

Phillips smiled. "You always did know when I was distracted…" he murmured. "I feel like I need to do something. To go somewhere… I don't know." Phillips looked around the pub as if the answer might jump out at him.

The two friends were only 30-years-old, but they'd aged a lot the last few years. He could see the fatigue in Phillips' heavy shoulders, the new wrinkles on his face from strain and hardship, but most of all he could see despair. Which is an awful thing to see in any man, let alone this paragon of strength and cheer.

"Yes!" said Joshua, with a determined fist landing on the table. "You need refreshment. You need perspective. And I know where you should go. I'm going with you."

❧

Several months later, the two friends met up in Israel. Phillips had traveled to Europe first, and Joshua had to tie up some loose ends in New York anyway. So they made the plan to spend the month of December in Israel. They spent the Holiday of Lights in Jerusalem. It was a Hanukkah neither of them would forget. It wasn't the typical American eight days of gifts for children, but there was a certain glimmer in the air.

On many evenings, they'd find themselves at local coffee houses talking and arguing happily with local rabbis. The Israelis were genuinely affected by the United States Civil War and the death of Lincoln; perhaps feeling their own empathy to a people's enslavement. Lincoln himself had used a passage from Ezekiel 7:23, "Make a chain: for the land is full of bloody crimes, and the city is full of violence." On March 4th, 1865, just a month before his assassination, Lincoln delivered his second inaugural address. Most people remembered the lighter side to the speech, the peaceful part of "with malice toward none, with charity for all." But later, there was a passage that had a darker tone, one of Ezekiel. Lincoln warned that the crimes of slavery might not be overcome until paid for in blood. "Fondly do we hope – fervently do we pray – that this mighty scourge of war may speedily pass away. Yet, if God wills that it continue, until all the wealth piled by the bond-man's two hundred and fifty years of unrequited toil shall be sunk, and until every drop of blood drawn with the lash, shall be paid by another drawn with the sword, as was said three thousand years ago, so still it must be said, 'the judgments of the Lord, are true and righteous altogether.'" To get to hear an eyewitness account of those years was something special, so Joshua and Phillips enjoyed a great deal of popularity in Jerusalem.

Afterward, the two friends traveled all over, following the steps of Abraham, Isaac, Jacob, Moses and Jesus. The Western Wall, the Church of the Holy Sepulcher, the Mount of Olives and Masada. Wherever the two friends would disagree theologically, they could certainly agree on the gravity of walking in these ancient places. The air was thick with history. America was so new. Europe felt new, in fact, compared to this!

But it was the day of Christmas Eve that touched Phillips the most. It was the least-grand event that they'd planned. In fact, the morning was spent doing chores around the home of their hosting family. They happily mucked out the stable, and then spread clean hay around the stalls with heavy pitchforks full of the fragrant, new hay. With bucket after bucket of water, they cleaned out and scrubbed the stables until they were gleaming.

As they spread the hay, the littlest girl of the household, about seven years old, came and chatted with them. Miriam was a calm child who took to walking about with her hands clasped behind her back, taking everything in. She didn't speak much, and her face was serene.

Without a word she had pitched right in. She'd carried a water bucket and started scrubbing right along with them. She even had her own child-sized pitchfork. Once in a while, they'd catch her throwing a forkful into the air, letting the hay rain down on her head. After a while, she climbed up onto a wall and watched them work, kicking her heels against the wall, a small smile playing on her face.

"Miriam," said Phillips, leaning on his pitchfork, taking a quick break, "why aren't you playing outside with your little friends?"

Miriam cocked her head, with her brown braids cascading down her back. "I like it in here, Mr. Brooks. The smell of hay, the horses whinnying, everyday work… I don't know. It's nice. And I saw a baby horse being born a few months ago!"

"But Miriam!" he said, "Why are you crying?" She'd suddenly had a few tears slide down her cheeks. But she hadn't moved, other than kicking her heels against the wall, carefree as always.

"Oh I'm not sad. It's just… touching, I think," she said in her child's voice. "When the colt was born, it was in the same stable that an old, ugly mare had died. She was ugly, but I loved her. I was sad that day. But… it was sweet that the little colt was born in that same place."

"Huh," said Phillips. "You're right. It is sweet."

He didn't say much the rest of the day. But Joshua had

his eye on him. He'd witnessed this little exchange between him and Miriam. It was a funny little talk. He had a peculiar notion that something important was happening. And Phillips had this look in his eye that he hadn't seen since they'd been at Harvard. He was deep in thought, like he was trying to figure out a puzzle. A puzzle that was challenging, but oh-so-intriguing to vanquish. The kind that teased your mind, giving little clues, but then bouncing back into the shadows of concealment making you all the more determined to figure it out. Very interesting indeed, thought Joshua to himself.

After an early dinner, they tacked the horses and decided to make a journey to Bethlehem. Miriam's parents had friends there that they were to stay with. After about two hours, they came to the town, situated on an eastern ridge of a range of hills, surrounded by terraced gardens.

Before dark, Phillips said to Joshua, "Let's ride out to the field where the shepherds saw the star!" Joshua grinned at him, fine with their theological differences again. Besides, if it was meaningful to Phillips, it was meaningful to him.

The large field had been fenced in along with a cave. "Why are all the Holy Places in caves here?" Phillips quipped. Joshua laughed; there *were* a lot of 'special' caves.

"Do you know, these are supposed to be the same fields from the story of Ruth and Boaz?"

"Of course I know that," Phillips said, making Joshua cackle.

As they passed, shepherds were still keeping watch over their flocks, leading them home to fold. The two friends stopped, their horses stood and shifted their feet back and forth, their tails slapping their sides. Both men took a moment to ponder and wonder about this place. The place where two huge events happened. And Bethlehem was by no means cute. It wasn't a classy place, one could say. The alleys were dark and dangerous. The people both 1800 years ago and currently, were not always overly friendly. Yet, a chosen site. One of goodness, kindness, new life. And miracles.

They slowly started back toward the town itself and they heard it. Oh the sound! A church nearby was filled to capacity and they were singing hymns. The songs floated out on the air to them. The two stopped again, letting the music soak into their minds and their souls.

"Splendid!" whispered Phillips. "I think this moment will sing in my soul for years to come."

❧

Late that night, after Joshua had gone to sleep, Phillips' mind was still buzzing with the experience. Those hymns. Those words. That place! It had changed him, somehow. And he felt more like himself than he had in a long, long time. He quietly got out of bed and went to the little desk in his room. He turned the wick of the lantern and lit a match. The small lantern lit the tiny room with its amber glow. Phillips uncorked the ink, took up his pen, dipped it, and began to write.

He whispered his heart-felt words as he wrote. "Oh little town of Bethlehem, how still we see thee lie; above thy deep and dreamless sleep the silent stars go by. Yet in thy dark streets shineth the everlasting light; the hopes and fears of all the years are met in thee tonight.

"How silently, how silently, the wondrous gift is given; so God imparts to human hearts the blessings of his heaven. No ear may hear his coming, but in this world of sin, where meek souls will receive him, still the dear Christ enters in."

He closed his journal, turned out the light and went to sleep.

శ్లీ

It would be years later that Joshua figured out what happened that day. First with Miriam and then with Bethlehem. He'd read a sermon by Phillips and there was a line that jumped out at him. It said, "It is while you are patiently toiling at the little tasks of life that the meaning and shape of the great whole of life dawns on you." Joshua was certain that that very day, while mucking out a horse stable, the meaning of the whole of life had dawned on Phillips. It wasn't in the huge events that we got the clearest view of life, it was in those small, sweet moments. Washing the dishes with your wife. Sitting on the porch of your grandma's house. Walking hand in hand with a love on a beach. Sledding down a hill. Those were the building blocks of life. Phillips was right.

Four years later, Joshua was walking home from services one night in December. A church nearby had its doors flung open and he enjoyed the beautiful music pouring out, a Christmas concert to be sure. A new song began and he stopped dead in his tracks as he heard the words, "O little town of Bethlehem, how still we see thee lie..." He listened to the entire hymn before his feet took him home and right to his desk.

With a quirky little smile, he uncorked the bottle of ink, picked up his pen, dipped it and wrote, "Dearest Phillips. I think I just heard a song you wrote!"

CHAPTER 15

"Thank so much for sharing that, Tom."

"Bruce." Honestly. I'm a moron.

"Anyway, that was incredible. I had no idea there was such history behind that little children's hymn," I said sincerely.

He laughed as if he knew exactly why I'd said Tom – that darn mustache – yet let me move on without humiliating myself any further than I'd already done. Bless him. "Yes. Many of the hymns have quite extraordinary stories behind them. You know, supposedly Phillips Brooks gave the new poem to his right hand man, Redner, a few days before Christmas in 1868. On the fly, Redner had to come up with the music for it. But it went off without a hitch and they had no idea that it would go beyond their own church. But it did; and as they say, the rest is history."

We said our goodbyes and my mind was racing with all this incredible content. I still had some time before my date with Drew, so... Wait, was it a date? I really could care less about the terminology. Me, him, steak, good. I sounded like a cave man. Oh well.

I worked at the conference table as the sun went farther down in the sky. When I looked up from the screen and my compelling story line that was developing, I spotted lights coming on in the twilight. You could really come to love this city. Some people crave nature, and I do at times, too. But the topography and energy of a city is inspiring.

I cranked out a few more pages and then with a crick in my back, I stood up, stretched a bit and went back to the hotel to change into something to eat steak in.

Right at 7 o'clock, I walked into Keens. I loved it immediately. The dark sculptured tin ceiling, dark wood walls, relieved with wall lamps, white table cloths, hundreds of old portraits, documents and letters framed on the walls, and large mullioned windows captured a fantastic ambiance. It had been established in 1885 and you could feel it.

Lover-of-history-that-I-am, I read up on Keens ahead of time. There's just too much stuff to share. It's a really cool place. But I must say, the ceilings lined with the large collection of clay pipes – I'm talking 90,000 – from Pipe Club members such as Teddy Roosevelt, General MacArthur, Liza Minelli and Babe Ruth are the best. Next to the steaks of course.

Drew was already at a table for two. I was planning my choice for dinner by the time I took off my coat, gave it to the hostess, and got to the table with red wine waiting for me.

"Hi, Coco. It's me, Drew."

"Sorry, was I distracted? I might've been drooling. I was thinking about what I was going to order."

"I figured. That's why I ordered an appetizer already." I might've fallen a little in love right then.

"My kinda guy!"

I sat down, smoothing out my dark gray sweater dress and patted down my curls a bit; it had been windy. I noticed his dark wine colored shirt, opened at the neck, and dress slacks. Now I had a couple of reasons to drool. He poured me a glass of wine and our appetizers arrived: lump crab cocktail and iceberg lettuce wedges with blue cheese dressing, tomatoes and bacon. Heaven.

"So did you have some good meetings today?" he asked.

"I did!" As we ate our appetizers, I filled him in on the

meetings with Tom Selleck and Wonder Woman. I was really getting around.

For dinner Drew ordered the sirloin and I ordered the Prime Filet with sides of creamed spinach and mushrooms. They were going to have to roll me out of there. I also got his opinion on some of the writing I was doing, what he felt would be a good approach to the narrative. Back at the office, I could bat around ideas with the other writers. I had narrowed it down to a couple of possible approaches and he gave some good input.

"Okay! Now you have to fill me in on your story," I said. "Where did we leave off? Oh yes, you ran off. Again."

"I actually want to take you somewhere else, first," he said with a grin.

"You have to tell me what relation you are to Willow, *first*. I know you're related. Throw me a bone."

His cheeky grin turned into a sweet smile. "She was my great-grandmother."

"Are you kidding?"

"Nope. I didn't get to know her for very long, she died when I was five. But I do remember her."

"Was Willow her real name?" I asked.

"No, it was Liesl. Liesl Taschner. But even as an elderly lady, she was tall and graceful. Slightly mysterious, too. It was easy to see why they called her Willow. It was a nickname her family gave her as a little girl. That's enough! There you go, now you have to follow me."

As we gathered our coats, he helped me put mine on. "It's novel leaving a restaurant *with* you."

"Ha. Ha. You're hilarious."

I was snickering. "Aren't I?" He made some sort of *pffft* sound.

We made our way down to 133 Mulberry Street. Little Italy started decorating for Christmas early, with lights and bows spanning the streets. If it was snowing, it would've looked a lot like Bedford Falls in *It's a Wonderful Life.* We walked into a Christmas wonderland. A store aptly named Christmas in Little Italy. We wandered around the store looking at all the ornaments, wreaths, and decorations.

"Hey, I found out something fun today," he said, looking up at a sprig of mistletoe. I got excited for a moment that maybe I'd get another kiss.

"Yeah! I found out the story behind mistletoe." So no kiss, then.

"What did you find out?" I asked, trying not to act disappointed.

"It's from the family of Sandalwood. It's actually a parasitic plant – it attaches itself to something else and is just about impossible to get rid of and it spreads wildly. The funniest thing is that in Old English it's misteltan. Tan means twig or branch. Mistel means dung because the seeds are carried everywhere from bird droppings."

"Wait, wait. You mean to tell me mistletoe means poop-branch?" I asked, snickering.

"Sure does," he said.

"I can totally see why you'd want to kiss someone under it."

"Well, I guess that part came from the fact that early Celts and Greeks thought it was sacred – kind of magical. So it's a maaaagical poop-branch," he said, making jazz hands.

I was laughing as I picked up a hand-painted Christmas ornament that depicted Little Italy at Christmas. I touched the pretty little red bow at the top. I could feel Drew watching me.

"You should get that," he said. "To remind you of this trip."

"That's a great idea. Or maybe this one of Bryant Park," I said. "I bet the ice-skating is so fun."

"It is," he said softly, moving closer so that he was right behind me as he reached to touch the Bryant Park ornament. I could smell his cologne and those little electric shocks came shivering along my spine from him being so close. "You know, those Celts and Greeks, they thought mistletoe was sacred, because only God's touch can make a new plant grow out of the death of winter. People of all different faiths feel that mistletoe represents hope, new life, safety... After a while, the little branches were hung over the doors of homes and barns to ward off enemies, and over babies' cribs to ward off evil and illness. Then in England it started to represent love. It makes sense, love is all about hope, life and security," he said softly, his deep voice whispery.

He'd stayed to my right and behind me a little, pressed up against me. I looked up at him, "It does make sense," I whispered. He looked down at my lips, I was most certainly looking at his.

But then he got a wolfish grin and said more loudly, "Then again, none of that would be sensible for someone who doesn't like Christmas. Right?" He cocked his eyebrow at me, daring me to disagree.

I was kind of speechless. So I just landed on, "Oh, you're terrible."

I could feel his laughter shaking him. He put his left arm around me and kissed my head, "Oh let's just get those two ornaments. Here, give them to me. I'm buying." I was still speechless as he took the ornaments right out of my hands and swept away.

"Thank you," I said cheerily as he handed me my little red bag with two ornaments inside. "Now what? We still have a lot to talk about and you *promised* to not run off this time."

"Oh, I'm not going anywhere. Come on, we have one more stop." He took my elbow and ushered me out the door. We walked farther down Mulberry Street to Da Nico.

We walked in and opted for a couple of seats at the bar. I was ruminating on Drew's comment about me not liking Christmas. Now, the Christmases I was discovering from Poppy and her father out at sea listening to the miraculous music; and Clement writing a poem that kindled sweet magic, and Rebekkah learning that forgiveness and love were just as wondrous as a sack of gold appearing in her stocking; and Thomas wrangling the courage to ask for forgiveness and build reconciliation that transformed into the first Christmas tree at Rockefeller... Well, now. They didn't bring out the Scrooge in me. They cut to the chase and illuminated the real meaning in all the celebration. They held the promise of hope and secret enchantments just around the corner. Hmm...

"Are you writing in your head?" asked Drew pulling his bar stool closer. "You look far away."

I smiled, "Yeah, I was. I have a lot to think about." I took a good look at him. We'd ordered dirty martinis and he took a drink of his. I wondered why he got involved in all this. It went back to the letter to Willow. But it was interesting that he'd jumped in with both feet and even did some research for me. Even after he'd slammed the door in my face. Interesting guy.

A guitarist sat down, and was playing a classical guitar

softly in the background. The martinis were ice cold, the music was golden, and the air itself sparkled with reflections of candlelight. It was an incredible moment.

"What?" he asked, my close scrutiny making him uncomfortable.

"So why did you decide to help me with all this? Especially after our first meeting ended so…"

"Abruptly?"

"Mm. Yes, abruptly. And suddenly you were enjoying my cocoa and French fries. And helping me a lot with this project."

He looked at me curiously, maybe chewing on his response?

"Yeah, hot cocoa." Did he mean hot Coco? I'm hilarious.

Despite my inward wittiness, I was captivated by the look in his eye. As a journalist, you learn to search for the meaning behind things. But I couldn't quite read his look.

"Coco, you remind me of someone. And when you came to my door, at first I was wary because of… well… you'll see. But my family has gone through a lot. It's not the first time a reporter came to my family's home."

"It's not?" I asked.

He moved closer, his look changing from curious to open, his voice changing from resonant to soft. "I was all set to never give you a second thought after I slammed the door. But the look in your eyes, it was shocking how much you suddenly reminded me of her. It was impossible to stay put. I saw you walk toward Third and I almost ran down the street until I saw you go into the Luncheonette. I thought I'd lost you."

"Who's *her*?" I asked, not sure of my grammar.

"Willow."

CHAPTER 16

Now we were getting somewhere. It was hard not being distracted by his closeness, but I wanted to see what he'd say.

"Willow?" I asked. "But you said she died when you were five. And I'm definitely not tall and willowy. Or mysterious."

"It's your eyes, your face. Not the colors and features, but she had this inner curiosity that made just being around her interesting." He put his hand on the back of my stool, coming close. "She was unafraid to try things and when she looked at you, you could feel that she wasn't looking *at* you, but *into* you. Like she was interested in who you were and was excited to learn. Even in photographs, you can see that intensity. You're the same."

"I like that."

"I do, too," he whispered. His hand on the back of the stool came to rest on the middle of my back, and he drew me toward him. Slowly, slowly our lips softly touched. Warmth spread through me and I melted into his kiss. I slid my hand up to the back of his neck, feeling his thick hair on my fingertips for the first time, and pulled him closer. After a delightfully long time, we rested our foreheads against each other for a moment.

Then I pulled away and collected myself. What were we doing here again? What's my name? I took a restorative sip of my martini. Hoo boy. That was some kiss. I stole a glance at him and was pleased to see some "collecting" of his own going on. He ran a hand through his hair and smiled to himself.

Getting back on track, I said, "You said yesterday you

had to get some things together. What's the mystery?"

"Well, it's funny you should say mystery," he said, grabbing his messenger bag and bringing it closer. He pulled out the letter to Willow and a small box. "We have some things to figure out."

"Ooh, I love a good puzzle. Okay, what do you know already?" I asked.

"Alright. Go ahead and see what's in the box."

"Let's see…" I said as I opened the lid to a small wooden box, plainly decorated with a vine around the edges.

"This is what my grandmother, Willow's daughter, gave me," he said.

Inside was a small key.

"A key?" I asked.

"Yes. And you helped uncover a big part of the mystery already," he said momentously.

"I did?"

"Mm hm. I think I might know what this key is going to find. All this time my copy of the letter had said the German's name was Marc. But yours said the German's name was Franz."

"Oh my god," I whispered, "Franz Marc the artist." *That's* what had been niggling at me all day! I wasn't an art historian by any means, but I happen to love the bright colors and work of artists like Kandinsky. Once, I was at the Guggenheim and saw the work of Franz Marc. I only remembered because it reminded me so much of Kandinsky. I'd loved it. But that was probably a decade ago. The colorful mural on the staircase at the WeWork office jogged that memory.

He was nodding, his eyes glittering. "I think Franz Marc

gave something of his to my great-grandfather, Herbert. I have no idea what, but this key is definitely a key to a safe deposit box." I'd always, *always*, wanted to get my hands on a good safe deposit box mystery. I've read far too much historical fiction...

"Why didn't your family get the contents of that box before now?" I asked, incredulously. A mystery *unsolved*? I wouldn't be able to function like that.

"Well," he said, "It's a long story. The most important thing, though, is that Herbert never made it home."

"He didn't?" I'd been so hoping that he did. But 1914 was just the beginning of the war. There were a lot of years and battles after that. It took so many lives, it was almost unfathomable. Especially in France, where many of the battles were fought and whose total population was much smaller than other countries. They almost lost an entire generation. The odds were good that Herbert wouldn't have made it.

Drew went on, "Then for some reason, even though he never returned from the war, the story of Herbert receiving something from a German soldier started circulating. It wasn't a big deal right then. But fast-forward twenty, twenty-five years and consorting with a German was a no-no. Then, don't forget Willow's real name."

"Liesl Taschner," I said. "German. McCarthyism," I said, putting it all together.

He nodded solemnly. "The 50s were ugly for our family. They had several friends wrongly accused of communist sympathies and they witnessed firsthand the reckless havoc of a paranoid nation. So they stuck up for them and suddenly the stories about Herbert started surfacing again. They were outlandish, getting more sensational every time the story was told."

I put my hand on his knee. He was lucky his family still had done so well, assuming his townhouse was a family home. Many who'd been accused of such things *didn't* fare so well.

I smiled, "So when you came into the picture, it was a natural fit for you to get into international law and human rights…"

"Exactly," he replied, smiling because I had made the link between his family history and his passion for his choice of career. "I'd always loved history and then I discovered the Monuments Men when I was in college. That sealed the deal. I love mysteries and standing up for what's right. It's been a good fit," he said, thoughtfully sipping his martini.

"But back to the key, our family had been afraid to even ask Willow about what Herbert had sent home from the front lines. And then World War II itself began so quickly, the exact details of the situation started to fade in the light of more urgent matters. They definitely never realized that Franz Marc was a well-known artist. I think they were just trying to survive and somehow the key and the package became forgotten. I think they started to assume that it was lost."

"But how did you get the key then?" I asked.

"My grandmother gave it to me when I won my first human rights trial. She just said to keep it safe. That certain things had been forgotten for a reason. But that one day, I would find where this key led."

"Wow! Talk about mysterious."

"I know," he said, raising his eyebrows. "Shortly after that she passed away. Then just a year or so ago, I was going through some old files and I found Herbert's letter. I'd heard about it, but I thought it had gotten lost or thrown away. Quite honestly, I didn't put the key and the letter together until I read your half of the letter yesterday."

"What are you thinking?" I asked. "How does it all fit together?"

"I believe that Willow gave this key to her daughter before she died. She may have been just as mysterious as my grandma was with me, so she might not have really known what it led to. I think that when we find this safe deposit box, we'll find what Franz handed to Herbert."

CHAPTER 17

The next day, I sipped a freshly brewed cup of coffee at Dylan's Candy Bar on Third Avenue at East 61st Street. Talk about colorful! The place was three floors of fun and deliciousness. But I'd come for a specific purpose. I wanted to know more about candy canes. So I met with a candy expert.

Funny thing was, I ended up at a Korean coffee shop called Grace Cafe in Korea Town, on 32nd Street, between Fifth and Sixth Avenue. Dylan's was just a fun candy stop that I'd been dying to try. I'd swallowed my own pride and bought a few Christmas presents, too.

Moxie had set up an appointment with a Korean baker who happened to have a penchant for Candy Canes. And he knew the history. Ho was right on time. The café was a delight with really good coffee, I mean really good, with a heart in the froth of my latte. The place had wonderful architecture and artwork. Couches, tall tables, low and long tables, all beckoned for you to come in for a chat with a friend or get some work done in an inspiring place.

It was impossible for me to tell how old Ho was, anywhere from mid-twenties to mid-fifties. I sat down at one of the tall tables and he dove right in.

"This is like the first candy canes," he said, eyes laughing, handing me a candy cane.

"Where are the stripes?" I asked, handling the pure white cane.

"Well, there are many legends around the candy cane. The earliest and most persistent legend is that the candy cane idea began with a choirmaster at Germany's Cologne Cathedral. Supposedly, he needed an idea to keep the kids quiet while the service was going on, after the children's choir had performed. He saw a white candy stick at the candy store and figured the hard candy would work since it takes a while to eat. Also, he asked the candy maker to bend the sticks – he'd then make a good illustration that the white would represent the sinless life of Christ and the crook would remind them of the shepherds that visited the Christ child."

"Handy," I commented.

Ho smiled and nodded. "Yes. And the idea took. Within a hundred years, white canes were adorning Christmas trees in Germany. But it wasn't until the 1920s that the candy canes got their red stripes." He brought out a large candy cane with the traditional stripes.

"A candy maker in Georgia, Bob McCormick, found a way to twist colors into hard candy. Supposedly he'd heard of an old, rather dubious Christian legend that during the time of Oliver Cromwell, when Christian celebrations were stopped by the Puritan leader, Christians would identify themselves to each other with the candy canes painted with three tiny red stripes indicating Father, Son and Holy Spirit, and one bold stripe representing the redemptive power of Christ. But, there was really no reason that legend was true, because even though Christmas celebrations were banned, formal worship was not, so they wouldn't have needed an identifying element such as the candy cane. But knowing this legend, and being a Christian himself, McCormick decided on this pattern. Plus, if you want to get really corny, if you turn it upside down, it's a 'J' for Jesus," he said, turning the cane on the table to make a J.

"Well," I said, "it's a good learning tool even if the legend isn't true."

"Yes, it is. And now, of course, candy canes come in every size, color and flavor. I myself, like the ones flavored by Starburst." I laughed, thinking it funny that this candy maker liked the commercial and fruity flavors.

"Thanks for sharing what you've learned. Do you know any other interesting tidbits about Christmas?" I asked, having some time to kill between appointments.

"Well, it's funny you should ask. There was a controversy in our youth group at our church on the origin of the Christmas song, *The Twelve Days of Christmas*." His eyes kept sparkling from the enjoyment of the topic.

"I haven't heard that one."

"Well, similar to the candy cane, I think perhaps Christians emphasized the sensational part of the story. But in the end, it's a wonderful learning tool."

"Okay. Tell me about it."

"Well, it started going around that The Twelve Days of Christmas was a secret code used by persecuted Catholics. Oh the stories give great detail about the persecution from the 1550s or so until 1829. But the Snopes article on this is excellent. It is urban legend. But the learning tool is still good. I think that the song's lyrics are so silly that someone somewhere thought it *had* to mean something else!" he laughed. "Anyway, it teaches that the love talked about in the song is the love of God, two turtle doves represent the Old and New Testaments. Three French hens are Faith, Hope and Charity, the Theological Virtues. Four calling birds are the Four Gospels. Five golden rings are the first five books of the Old Testament, the Pentateuch." He was ticking down the list with his fingers. I was amazed he could remember it by heart. Maybe it really was a good learning tool.

"Six geese a-laying are the six days of creation. Seven swans a-swimming are the seven gifts of the Holy Spirit. Eight maids a-milking are the eight beatitudes. Nine ladies dancing are the nine Fruits of the Holy Spirit. Ten lords a-leaping are the Ten Commandments. Eleven pipers piping are the eleven faithful apostles. And twelve drummers drumming are the twelve points of doctrine in the Apostle's Creed."

Ho banged his hand on the table with a flourish, grinning ear to ear.

I laughed, "Well done! I can see where it's a good story, but I think I'd feel pretty dubious if I read that. Seems like a stretch here and there…"

He winked, "Indeed it does. But like I said, good learning tool."

We said goodbye and like all the rest, I promised I'd send him the article when completed. I thought of all these people I was meeting. Since most of them, I felt, had become friends, I started to get the beginning of a fun idea.

I looked at my watch and made my way downtown. I took a cab then walked to the corner of Reade and Broadway, down by City Hall. I needed to take a tour of City Hall some time. A lot of history was made there! I looked around at the buildings before I met my next appointment. I saw the Freedom Tower. Funny how I still missed the World Trade Center Buildings so much – they would've been *right there*. It was a very odd feeling that one act of terror could change the landscape so much. But I really loved the Freedom Tower. I needed to go there and visit the 9/11 Memorial as well. I was sure I'd cry the entire time. I heard the memorial is incredibly well done. I took a deep breath and walked into the Starbucks.

This time, I was the first one to the appointment. I was meeting a Mr. Geoffrey Reynolds. I didn't know anything about him, except that I had gotten a cryptic message from Drew early this morning that he wanted me to meet someone. A friend of his. And that this meeting would be great for my story, but also might shed light on my "Christmas issues." I almost choked as I read the words. Issues. I don't have *issues.* Sheesh. Ya tell a guy you don't like Christmas and look what happens.

I had sent an email right back that said, "Sure I'll meet your friend. Thanks! But watch it, Buddy. I'll give *you* issues if you're not careful." I could almost hear his cackle from my hotel. *Issues. Pfft.*

After I got a coffee and sat down – and was pondering these issues I don't have – I saw my appointment walk in. I have no idea what made me just know he was the man I was meeting. But I did. And he spotted me right away, as well. He signaled that he'd go get a coffee first and I nodded. It gave me a minute to think. He was a little, old, wizened, but spritely African-American gentleman. He was bent over a bit, but somehow managed a little skip in his step. He had a light covering of black and gray hair on his head and he held a cane. He talked with the cane like my grandpa used to do. Waved it around like an extension of his hands, gesturing in perilous form. I smirked as the people near him in line shuffled around to give him a little extra room.

"Hello, Mr. Reynolds. It's lovely to meet you," I said, standing and extending my hand as he tottered to the table after he got his coffee.

He took my hand in his and warmly responded, "Oh my dear. The pleasure is all mine. And I can see why our mutual friend was so insistent that I meet with you today."

"What do you mean?" I asked, curiosity piqued.

"I think that our meeting is one of those rare, oh, shall we say, meetings of the mind. Kindred spirits perhaps." I pretty much felt my eyes start to sparkle more. I liked him a lot. Then as he fussed with his coffee, he murmured something like, "And I think he's pretty hot for her…"

I snorted and tried to cover it up with a cough. He looked up at me and squinted, judging the dubious nature of my cough. I hurried on, "So! Drew tells me that you're a friend and I assume he told you that I'm collecting not only the history of Christmas Traditions, but also the human interest stories behind them. Every event wasn't just an event. It started with one person, one idea. *That's* what I want to capture."

"Truer words were never spoken, my dear. Well, my grandfather was close friends with a reporter in his day. In fact, a journalist not unlike yourself, I should think. My grandfather would tell us about him and especially about the unusual friendship they formed. Back in those days, although slavery had come to an end officially, and although there were many black men and women in New York City at the time, it was unusual for a white man to befriend a young black boy. But they had a special bond. And that's the story I wanted to tell you. You'll know some of the story, I'm sure. But like you said, it takes one person, one idea, to change the course of events…and make history.

CHAPTER 18

New York City
September 20, 1897

Oh it was a hot one. Well, not like August, but it was the hottest September in New York City history. He liked it though, the winters could be really harsh in the big city. So a warmer, kinder September might just make the winter a little more bearable.

Louis' father had been trying to get the ten-year-old to take his reading more seriously, but the little boy just didn't see the point. That is, until he'd heard about the editorial. *The Editorial*. It was big news in their little school. The boys and girls were on pins and needles waiting to read the reply. A daring young girl gathered the courage to ask an authority if there really was a Santa Claus.

It was an important debate amongst him and his friends. Sometimes they'd resort to fisticuffs to decide. But he was a big kid, already earning the moniker, Big Lou. So he'd rein in the debaters. But you couldn't decide a thing like that with fists! No, sir. This needed an expert. This needed the final determination from an informed adult.

Now, Louis was not exactly an authority on the issue, either. Really, Santa didn't come every year to the Buckley home. In fact he didn't show up most years. But there was just this gnawing inside Lou that needed to know for sure!

Lou and his family had moved to the North after he attended segregated schools in North Carolina. They landed in Connecticut first, and finally the city. After school, Lou would do odd jobs all over the place to earn some extra pennies. He was industrious all right. And this city was full of opportunities. He was always rubbing his hands together in great anticipation of what each day held for him.

That day, he took his place near Reade and Broadway. Just outside *The Sun*. Which just happened to be the penny paper that had this intriguing question from another industrious sort of person, the question of the truth of Santa. He'd like to meet her one day, that Virginia O'Hanlan. That kind of moxie was something he admired. In fact, he was ruminating on that moxie while he was shining the living daylights out of the black shoes in front of him.

"Big Lou! How are you, today?"

"Oh, I'm doing really well," he responded while giving the shiny shoes a slap with his towel. They shined like a mirror. He could even see his big grin mirrored in the toes.

"You look deep in thought. Like you have a good secret or something fun to look forward to."

"Indeed I do, Mr. Church!"

"Well let's have a chat about it. Come on, I'll buy us a lemonade." Mr. Church and Big Lou made quite the odd couple. But they'd formed an interesting friendship. They walked around the park opposite City Hall and Mr. Church bought them each a lemonade from a vendor. There was a petite Italian nearby with an accordion and a little monkey dancing. Mr. Church popped a penny in his direction and the monkey leaped on the penny and took it to his master. Both the master and the little monkey tipped their hats, making Big Lou chuckle.

"Thanks for the lemonade! It's perfect on a warm day like this," said Lou.

"It is, isn't it? So what's on your mind?"

"Well, there is quite the debate going on at school. And I am excited about it," he responded earnestly. "And you'll never guess what that debate is about, you just never will."

Mr. Church laughed amicably; he enjoyed Lou's enthusiasm. There wasn't anything Lou wasn't enthusiastic about. But this must have really captured his imagination because he was fairly buzzing and humming with anticipation. "I think you're right! And you've got my curiosity good and piqued, I don't mind saying."

"It's about Santa Claus and that editorial question from Virginia O'Hanlon at *The Sun*! Is there a Santa Claus?"

Mr. Church laughed some more, "That's what's gotten you so excited?"

"Oh yes. It's a heated debate at school." Lou suddenly remembered that Mr. Church was an adult, of course, and perhaps he thought this a silly thing. He felt sheepish and looked down at his shoes, trying to figure out how to change the subject.

Mr. Church didn't miss much, and he definitely caught Lou's sudden change of demeanor. He squinted at him, reading him. "Lou? That's an excellent question, isn't it? I think it's one we would all like an answer to."

Lou looked over at his friend, his studious face, his hands linked behind his back like a professor deep in thought, and his kindness that seemed a part of every gesture. Lou's sheepishness vanished on the spot. Mr. Church was a different sort of adult. Big Lou thought he might like to be that sort of adult one day.

"It is, Mr. Church." So Lou talked about the lively debates at school, his own thoughts and hopes, and even how his family felt about it. He brought up one point that Mr. Church found poignant indeed.

"You see, Mr. Church, my mother isn't a very oh, fanciful type person. She likes to talk about evidence. And things you can see. Santa can actually be a sore topic for her. I can't figure out why. But you know, Santa doesn't come every year at our house. I figure – if he's real – he's got to be busy some of the years, right? So it just makes sense that sometimes he doesn't have the helpers he needs, or something. But I just can't put my finger on it, there's something important and real about it."

◈

Mr. Church looked at Lou, watching his thoughts forming, his furrowed brow, how he'd subconsciously clasped his hands behind his back just as he'd done. He smiled to himself. Francis Church had laughed when he saw that editorial question, and couldn't fathom what had gotten into his bosses at *The Sun* to print it! He felt for the poor slob who'd be assigned to that one. But he did have to admit, he liked how it had inspired Lou. And his friends.

"Right, Mr. Church?"

"I'm sorry, Lou, I missed the question. What did you say?"

"Life is hard and we work to make ends meet every day. I just think that without Santa and his kind of surprises and mystery, life just wouldn't be as beautiful."

"Lou! You should be a writer. You have a profound mind, son," said Mr. Church, stunned by the depth of this young man. He caught a glimpse of the man he'd be one day.

"Oh no, sir. I'm going to be a policeman." Mr. Church grimaced a bit, there weren't men of any kind of color on the police force. In fact, they'd just allowed the first Italians on the force. Not to mention they didn't make much money and the detectives didn't work on a case unless they were "paid" to by the victim's families. The word bribe was never used, but that's what it was. Although, Teddy Roosevelt was making some big reforms. He made changes for promotion based on merit and the enforcement of all laws for the past two years as Police Commissioner. He'd even hired the first woman on the force and created the first finger printing department. Mr. Church was still a little skeptical about the veracity of finger printing, but maybe... The city was still concerned that all Teddy's reforms would go back to the way things were before, since he left to be the Assistant Secretary of the Navy back in April. They'd just have to wait and see.

This time it was Lou's turn to read Mr. Church. He knew what he was thinking. "Don't worry, Mr. Church. The police force won't go back to what it was. Things are changing! I'll make it. You'll see."

"That is something I'm certain of, Lou. Keep working. You'll do whatever you set your heart out to do. And... don't ever forget that wonder about Santa Claus. It's powerful," he said, looking at his watch on the chain in his pocket. "I have to get going, now. Thanks for the talk!"

"And thanks for the lemonade!"

The two friends parted ways. Lou finished his day with a couple of customers, and then headed home.

Mr. Church went up to his office. He was finishing up a story he'd been putting together for a couple of weeks. He wrote the last word and stretched his arms up over his head in a big cat-like stretch. He rested his clasped hands behind his head and reclined back from his typewriter. He started forming lists of what to accomplish in the remaining hours of the day. He hadn't checked his box where the secretaries inserted their next jobs handed down. His right hand lazily grasped the thin pile of papers. He sifted through them and then saw a small hand-written letter fall out of the pack. It was short, and had neat, carefully written sentences.

"Well I'll be…" he said out loud to no one else but himself. There on his desk, obviously having made the rounds to several other desks before landing on his, was the letter from Virginia O'Hanlon. The very one his friend Lou had been telling him about: Was there really a Santa Claus?

❧

That night, Louis lay in bed, his hands clasped behind his head, gazing up at the shadows and beams of light playing on his ceiling. That talk with Mr. Church really got his mind going. He needed to start making plans for his future. He'd already been saving some pennies as he made them. Most of them he gave toward the family expenses, everyone was doing what they could. But he'd keep a couple here and there. He fell asleep with a grin on his face and dreams of possibilities dancing around in his mind.

The next morning as he went down to breakfast, his mother was slamming around pots and pans as she put together the family breakfast. Lou eyed his sister and she gave a wide-eyed, slight shake of her head that said, "Don't mess with Mama!" Oh… his heart sank a bit. It was one of those days. So they ate in silence, their father having gone to work already.

Their mother heard the quick, almost silent exchange between Lou and his sister. "What are you talking about now? You are not talking about that dumb editorial in *The Sun* again, are you?" Lou had learned long ago how to make his face a blank slate. His sister was not so lucky.

"Cynthia Buckley! You just stop that chatter right now. There is no such thing as Santa! There I said it! Now get some real thoughts, real plans in your head this minute. You get to school, now!"

Lou helped his sister down from the chair that was a little too tall for her short legs. He patted her shoulder. At least she didn't cry. They'd both learned that tears weren't helpful around their mother, either.

"Louis! And I don't want you talking one more peep about being a police officer again! You just won't be able to change things, so you need to start thinking clearly about it now. You'll only be disappointed." Why did she have to take those cheap shots at his dreams? He'd only told them a little about his talk with Mr. Church yesterday. He probably shouldn't have said one word. He got his sister out the door, and then forgot his books upstairs. He quietly ran up and tiptoed back down. He had to pass the kitchen where his mother still sat.

She was looking out the window, an incredibly sad look on her face. Not one tear appeared, though. She had never cried in front of him. She looked down at her apron. He noticed it, maybe for the first time. She always wore it, so it seemed part of her more than something she wore. She fingered the bottom hem. He noticed burn marks on a couple of edges, and the blue of the fabric had faded so that it was now light gray. It was stained on the front and he was sure it had been scrubbed approximately three thousand times, but to no avail. Before she could catch him, he quickly flew out the door.

That day, he walked up the steps of his school, his head a little heavy, his shoulders carrying a burden he hadn't felt before. Maybe it *was* too much to think the New York City police would change. Maybe the best he and his sister could hope for was to just keep mama not angry. He'd once hoped they could make her happy. But it didn't look like that was ever going to be possible. And he had a spelling test today. Wonderful.

When he opened the door, something incredible had happened. The air was bursting with something exciting. It was like a circus had come to town, handed out candy to everyone, and brought puppies to boot. Every kid was running to and fro, yelling, some cheered with their fists raised in the air in triumph, and the smiles. The smiles and laughter were something he'd cherish his entire life.

His friend Joseph ran up to him and almost screamed, "It came out! The letter! *The Sun* ANSWERED Virginia!"

"What?" he gasped. Joseph had thrust the paper into his hands. Sure enough, an editor responded. His heart was thumping practically out of his chest. His hands were sweaty all-of-a-sudden. He pulled over to the side, put his head down, and read the words he'd never forget. At the top of the paper was *The Sun* title and its slogan "It Shines for All." His eyes shot down to read the letter.

Is There a Santa Claus?

We take pleasure in answering at once and thus prominently the communication below, expressing at the same time our great gratification that its faithful author is numbered among the friends of The Sun:

Dear Editor: I am 8 years old. Some of my little friends say there is no Santa Claus. Papa says, "If you see it in The Sun, it is so. Please tell me the truth; is there a Santa Claus? -Virginia O'Hanlon, 115 West Ninety-fifth Street.

Virginia, your little friends are wrong. They have been affected by the skepticism of a skeptical age. They do not believe except they see. They think that nothing can be which is not comprehensible by their little minds. All minds, Virginia, whether they be men's or children's are little. In this great universe of ours man is a mere insect, an ant, in his intellect, as compared with the boundless world about him, as measured by the Intelligence capable of grasping the whole of truth and knowledge.

Yes, Virginia, there is a Santa Claus. He exists as certainly as love and generosity and devotion exist, and you know that they abound and give to your life its highest beauty and joy. Alas! How dreary would be the world if there were no Santa Claus. It would be as dreary as if there were no Virginia. There would be no child-like faith then, no poetry, no romance to make tolerable this existence. We should have no enjoyment, except in sense and sight. The eternal light with which childhood fills the world would be extinguished.

Not believe in Santa Claus! You might as well not believe in fairies! You might get your papa to hire men to watch in all the chimneys Christmas Eve to catch Santa Claus, but even if they did not see Santa Claus coming down, what would that prove? Nobody

216

sees Santa Claus, but that is no sign that there is no Santa Claus. The most real things in the world are those that neither children nor men can see. Did you ever see fairies dancing on the lawn? Of course not, but that's no proof that they are not there. Nobody can conceive or imagine all the wonders there are unseen and unseeable in the world.

You may tear apart the baby's rattle and see what makes the noise inside, but there is a veil covering the unseen world which not the strongest man, nor even the united strength of all the strongest men that ever lived, could tear apart. Only faith, fancy, poetry, love, romance, can push aside that curtain and view and picture the supernal beauty and glory beyond. Is it all real? Ah, Virginia, in all this world there is nothing else real and abiding.

No Santa Claus! Thank God! He lives and he lives forever. A thousand years from now, Virginia, nay, ten times ten thousand years from now, he will continue to make glad the heart of childhood. –Francis P. Church, editor.

"Well I'll be," said Lou out loud. Mr. Church? He was speechless. He fought the lump in his throat and surreptitiously wiped what felt like a tear at the corner of his eye. "Well now. That changes things."

ॐ

Three months later, it was Christmas morning. Lou's

mother was in a sour mood, of all days. His father was trying to lighten the feeling in the house. It was a sparse Christmas, to be sure, but Lou's heart was full anyway. Before they had their meager breakfast, he and his sister brought out a carefully wrapped box. It was wrapped in newspaper, with a red bow on it. Even without shiny decorations or velvety ribbons, it was glorious. He and his sister exchanged a nervous glance.

"Mama? We have something for you." She shot a wary look to her husband, but he had no idea what was going on. He just shrugged.

"Just open it," said Lou with a smile.

"Well, I don't know what you've done. I hope you haven't been wasting our money," she grumbled. But he noticed that her fingers carefully, almost lovingly, unfastened the box. Her hand caressed the box and she opened the top. Inside there was a layer of white tissue paper. She carefully pulled that off and gasped, her hand covering her mouth, her fingers quivering. "But how…" she murmured, her voice light and wondrous. Lou could feel his grin growing to a full-fledged smile. He heard his father blow his nose, a sure sign he'd been touched, too.

His mother's quivering fingers pulled out a vibrant, sky-blue apron. Thick lace edged the bottom hem, nice wide strips came out from the sides, sure to make a lovely big bow when tied at the back. Little white polka-dots played all around the soft yet sturdy material. She ran to the mirror in the hall and pulled it over her head and tied the bow in the back. She came back in the room, looking ten or twenty years younger. Her smile was… sweet. He'd never seen his mother looking sweet before. He was rather flummoxed at the change. But his father wasn't.

His father went to her and put his big arms around her, pulling her toward him in a giant embrace. All of her cares, her worries, and her sour mood seemed to simply fall off her shoulders. And she sobbed. Lou and his sister clasped hands, unsure what was going on and not completely certain that they hadn't done something wrong. Then their father saw them and laughed heartily.

"Come here!" They ran to their parents and enjoyed a hug bigger than any of them had ever experienced.

Just then, there was a knock at the door and a loud voice yelled, "Delivery!" Lou made it to the door first, almost slamming into it, he'd run so fast. When he opened the door, there was no one there. But his sister, peeking out right behind him, said, "Look!"

At their feet, was a large box marked, "Buckley Family. Merry Christmas." Their father brought in the package. Inside was a large turkey, two big rounds of fresh bread, vegetables, potatoes and two pies! It was a feast! At the bottom of the package, Lou noticed a small envelope. The family was already in the kitchen, so he pulled out the envelope and sat down in the living room.

He carefully opened the blue envelope. Inside was a letter on thick, nice paper. It felt good in his hands.

> *Dear Lou,*
> *Thank you. You helped me find a voice for myself and for the city. Your spirit is contagious. Your love of your family, and your secret surprise for your mother, that I was fortunate enough to participate in, has made me a better man. Merry Christmas.*
> *Your personal Santa Claus, and friend,*
> *Mr. Church*

Lou folded the letter and put it in his pocket. With a grin on his face, he thought of saving up for his mother's apron, then asking Mr. Church where to buy something like that. Mr. Church had asked his wife, and one day they went shopping. Lou knew the moment he laid eyes on that polka-dot blue apron, it was destiny. Mr. Church had tried to help purchase it, but Lou had saved his own money and wanted to do it himself. Seeing the importance of it, Mr. Church nodded sagely.

It had been hard keeping that box from his mama's eyes! He and his sister had to move it almost every day to keep her from finding it as she cleaned. Lou listened to the giggling in the kitchen, the plans for the turkey, a light-hearted argument about making mashed or pan-browned potatoes. It was the best Christmas he'd ever had. And he was convinced more than ever, there really was a Santa Claus.

He walked to the kitchen and joined in the fun.

CHAPTER 19

"So you really are Big Lou's grandson?" I asked.

He nodded, eyes bright. "I am indeed."

"And did he make the police force?"

He nodded again. "Sure did! All six feet, three inches and two-hundred eighty pounds of him! Heh, heh, heh," he laughed. "He was the first African American police officer in New York City. Sworn in on March 6, 1911. Earned a lot of respect, too. Saved an officer's life and that got him noticed and respected. He got into the Sergeant's Academy and he was the first NYPD black lieutenant. I always think that maybe he ended up as the parole commissioner, working with youths in Harlem, because of that whole Santa thing and his friendship with Church. I don't know. Maybe," he said, eyes twinkling.

"How about Virginia? What happened with her afterward?" I asked.

"Well, she went to Hunter College and received her Masters at Columbia. She taught in the New York City school system for over 47 years! And do you know, when she retired, *The Sun* was still running her letter and Church's response every Christmas."

"Well, I love this backstory with Church and Buckley and Virginia. I can't thank you enough." We said goodbye and I told him about the idea I'd had yesterday. He thought it was a splendid plan. We walked out together and parted ways. I watched him walk down the block, enthusiastically swatting at two pigeons with his cane. I shook my head, smiling to myself.

I made my way back toward my hotel. I decided to take the 4 / 5 train uptown. I hadn't done the subway yet. I found my way down all the stairs to the labyrinth below the streets and it was easy to see the signs for the 4 / 5 and 6 trains. I bought a MetroCard and swiped it as I went through the turnstile. Unfortunately I had started to barge through and rammed full-force into the unyielding turnstile. I apparently missed that the stupid machine read, "Please swipe again." I was pretty sure I'd have a bruise on my thighs for that one. I swiped again and it decided to let me through this time. I suppressed the urge to kick it.

I waited on my platform, reasonably sure I was in the right place. Then I watched as two college students carried – yes, carried – a queen-sized mattress up to the platform. That would be fun. The train pulled into the station and I got onto the train, a little excited to see how these kids would get the mattress on the train. It put up a good fight, but they managed to wrestle it on. I wasn't too sure I'd want to sleep on a mattress that had traveled by subway...

I got out at 42nd Street and walked over to the *The Pod 39* at 39th. The rooftop bar at my hotel was the perfect place to get some thoughts together. I walked out onto the roof to a beautiful scene. There were cushioned benches all around the edges. There were brick arches here and there that gave the open space some beautiful architectural highlights. You add some twinkle lights and a glass of wine? A girl could get used to this.

As I sipped a little Pinot Noir, I looked up some background information on *The Sun*. It was one of the first newspapers to report crimes and personal events such as suicides, deaths, and divorces. It was significant because it was about ordinary people. Benjamin Day as editor-in-chief was the first to hire reporters to go out and collect news stories. Before then, papers relied on stories coming to them, writing book and theater reviews, etc. It was the beginning of what really got my heart pumping about journalism. It's all about *the people* that make the story.

I got my notes together, sent some things off to my Spidey-editor, and felt quite accomplished. I made a couple of calls about the plan that I was developing and then since I hadn't heard from Drew, left him a message and went to my room to hop in the shower.

When I got out, I found a text from Drew, asking me to meet him at a bank in his neighborhood. I quickly dressed and got a cab uptown. Look at me using the New York lingo!

I pulled open the door of the Citibank at 79th Street and First Avenue and walked in.

"Ha ha ha! Why the sour face?" asked Drew, between laughs.

"Oh, I wanted the bank to be a big old thing, still here from the 1800s and all mysterious. Not a CitiBank. *So* not mysterious."

"Well! Let me tell you about my adventure," he said.

I got excited. Maybe he'd found some interesting tidbits about his family, maybe he'd been all over the city hunting down facts and loose ends all day…

He shook his head, "I'm just kidding. I called the family attorney. He had the information."

"Bah!" I said, disgusted with the normalcy of it.

Still snickering, we walked over to the manager and headed toward the safe deposit boxes. Meanwhile, Drew filled me in that the family had indeed owned a couple of safe deposit boxes over the years. He'd been instructed to move the contents at one point, to this location. Drew had the legal license for any and all family documentation, and since he had the key, we were all set.

We got to the box, and Drew pulled out a large briefcase, opened the box, and kill-joy-that-he-is, emptied the box right into his briefcase without looking at anything!

"Wh- Wh- Wh-," I sputtered.

More laughing on his part. Horrible man. "Come on! Let's go back home and look at everything. I have a bottle of wine and dinner will be ready in an hour or so." Well, since he put it that way...

We walked back toward his place. My eyes wandered toward the flowers outside a small florist. "I'm getting these!" I said, drawn to the gorgeous colors. I picked a large bunch of flowers; orangey-red alstroemeria and red roses mixed with light green and red berries.

Back at his kitchen, he uncorked a nice white wine while I put the flowers in a vase. He got some cheeses and olives and put them on a wood paddle to serve. We sat down at the bar stools in his kitchen, touched glasses and drank the dry pinot grigio. Wow. The scent of the flowers, the tang of the wine, the salty cheese, the ridiculously good-looking man next to me... This was exceptional. I realized people didn't live like this all the time; walking all over a thriving city, making new friends, experiencing new things every week, every day. But it was really something. Something not drowsy. I'll take it.

I quickly filled him in on my chat with Ho, and everything he explained about the candy canes. And then I relayed the story of Big Lou, the backstory of a life affected by the Virginia letter. I bet there were hundreds, maybe thousands more lives affected similarly.

"Don't you wish you could've been there the day that Virginia's letter hit the schools?" I asked enthusiastically.

"Oh yeah. It would've been unequivocal validation."

"Sure would! Hey, you know how my parents felt about Santa. How about your family?" I asked.

"Oh we all loved it. My grandpa used to dress up as Santa on Christmas Eve. He'd disappear and in a while we'd hear the doorbell ring. It was Santa with a bag of presents. My little sister used to be scared to death of Santa, though. We figured out one year that it was really Grandpa."

"How? How did you know?"

"Well, besides the skimpy beard with elastic showing," he said, smiling fondly, "he forgot to put on his black gloves this one year. The day before he'd burned his hand pretty badly and still had the big bandages on."

"Aw! Poor guy! His secret was out," I said.

"I know. I felt awful. I'd known it was him for a while, but when my sister pointed out the bandaged hand and exclaimed, 'It's just Grandpa!' I thought my heart would break. He was so crestfallen."

"That's really sweet. So you opened presents on Christmas Eve?" I asked.

"Yep. The extended family got together that night and we all opened our presents. I still remember being a kid and going to bed early at my grandparents' house. I could hear all the adults talking and laughing late into the night. Then our parents would come and wrap us up in blankets and carry us home. The next morning we opened presents from Santa and the immediate family and then have a big breakfast."

"That sounds really nice," I said. Hmm. For a guy who supposedly didn't like Christmas, he had an awful lot of good memories…

We decided to get down to business and finally find out

about the contents of that safe deposit box. We took our wine back to his oatmeal colored, soft couch in the living room. He went to the front door and grabbed his briefcase.

He cleared off the coffee table and said, "Ready?"

"Oh yeah."

Drew carefully slid out the contents of his briefcase onto the table. There were packets of papers, a few books that looked like ledgers or something, one set of coins that reminded me of my grandpa who collected coins, and one thick packet in a manila 5x7 envelope.

"I think that's it!" he exclaimed, as I simultaneously said, "No gun. Damn." He gave me a wary look as we both edged closer to the table.

Drew picked up the packet and drew out a small, dark maroon leather book. The pages were dog-eared, as if it had been riffled through many, many times. The spine was still intact, a nice smell of old leather drifted from it. He carefully placed it on the coffee table between us and opened it to the first page.

Sure enough, inside the front cover, written in script on a diagonal was a capital "F" with the squiggle of an "S" next to it. Then "Marc." The M in Marc looked a little like the pi-sign. I quickly googled Franz Marc's signature and sure enough…

"Oh my gosh," I whispered as I held up the identical signature on the book and on my phone. I got shivers as we slowly leafed through the little book.

"Look at this!" Drew whispered. Somehow both of us needed to whisper at this amazing moment. It was a sketch of what looked like three horses, then one of a single horse. At the very end of the book was a sketch with the hint of colors. Drew said in a squeaky voice, "It's Fighting Forms.

It's one of his final major works!"

I recognized the colors, it was the one that I'd been reminded of when I saw that bright mural at WeWork.

"I did some research on him," said Drew, pulling out a few papers. "I mostly looked up the time he was in the war. He enlisted in 1914 as a cavalryman, but by 1916 he was drawn to military camouflage. He'd paint canvas covers to hide military equipment." Drew smiled as he looked closely at his notes, "He even used a variety of styles, from Manet to Kandinsky. He thought the Kandinsky style would be the most effective to disguise artillery from planes overhead."

I picked up the little book and carefully thumbed through. Drew went on, "The saddest part, though, was that the German government decided to pull noteworthy artists from the ranks of the military front, to secure the future of the German culture. Marc was on that list. But he was hit by a shell before those orders could reach him."

"Oh my god, Herbert had been right. Maybe he really did see something of that premonition in Franz Marc's eyes when they met," I said.

"Maybe. It's still a wonder that he'd pass this on to a stranger. A stranger in the enemy army no less."

"Mm hm," I said, taking a sip of wine while I thought about that exchange. "I don't know. Sometimes people get an inkling that a gesture is just the right thing, at just the right moment. Like your grandmother giving you the key, knowing that you'd put it all together when the stars aligned properly. Maybe it was a similar thing between Marc and Herbert. *Something* was certainly working to bring you and your career, Willow and her Herbert, and even me here to this time and place, all together…"

"Yeah, maybe," he said thoughtfully. "It certainly was a

remarkable moment in history. I bet there were grand gestures up and down the front lines that night."

I'd uncovered a lot of grand gestures this past week, working on this story. Lives that were touched and changed because of the courage and innovation of a person. I thought through some of those stories, places, and events, and how all of them centered around Christmas. I was definitely feeling like I was getting a better picture of Christmas. Maybe being The Christmas Journalist wasn't so bad after all... But I wouldn't be saying that out loud.

"Where'd you go?" asked Drew softly, having come closer on the couch next to me, so that our legs were touching. He was very nicely, much closer. I could smell his cologne and was close enough to look at where his button-down shirt was opened at the collar. I love the five o'clock shadow, neck and collarbone on a man. Really hot. My stomach was doing flip-flops.

"I... was thinking of all the great stories we dug up this week," I said, talking softly since he was so near.

"Your voice sounds like you're wrapping up," he said with a concerned brow.

"Well, I am almost finished. I guess it has to come to an end."

"No it doesn't," he said as he put my glass of wine down, and pulled me to him. Our lips met and our arms naturally fell into place around each other. He pulled away a little, both of us slightly out of breath. My hand was on his chest, feeling his muscles underneath. He whispered huskily, "Stay with me." I melted into another long kiss.

And my phone rang.

My phone never rings. Suddenly, I was brought back to real life. Real problems. On top of that, it was the ring I associated with my mother. Impeccable timing.

"Is it your editor?" he asked.

"Worse. My mother." I sighed exasperatedly and said with resignation and a slight whine, "I'd better get it. She never calls, so…" I got up and went to my bag across the room, my phone perched on top.

"Hello, Mom," I said. "I can't talk long, I'm in the middle of something." I looked back over at Drew and winked at him. "Everything okay there?"

She talked for several minutes. Nothing was wrong, she was just checking in. It was like I was suddenly back in their house, with the salt-less meals and my dad's paper-turning the only sound I could hear. She wanted to know if I'd been mugged or anything, was I eating too many rich foods, was I basically having too much fun, dreaming too much. I felt sick. It was like I was having this amazing and wonderful dream, only to wake up to a drab, black and white world. Wait. Like Dorothy and the Wizard of Oz. I was at the end, waking up back in Kansas. Damn it. We hung up and I stood there a second longer.

"Oh no you don't," said Drew, suddenly appearing right next to me.

"Don't what?" I said.

"You're going to do a Cinderella on me, aren't you?"

"I.. Well, I…"

"Put your purse down." I did. "That was your mother. Is everything okay? No heart attacks or anything?"

"Everything is fine. She was just checking up on me," I said, with a long-suffering grimace.

He laughed. "And what? She brought you back to reality?"

I gave him a quizzical look. "How did you know?"

"You had the same look on your face that I used to get at the end of vacation and I knew I had to go back to school, tests, and homework."

I laughed. "Yeah, it felt a lot like that," I said, running my hand through my hair. I wanted to stay. I wanted to stay with Drew, more specifically, but it was complicated. God, I hate the word *complicated*.

"Look. Let's just have dinner. Come on! I can smell that it's almost done," he said with a boyish grin that made me happy and sad at the same time. Boy, I really didn't want to leave. I followed him downstairs and we ate a spaghetti dinner with garlic bread and Caesar salad. After dinner, we decided we had one more night together, tomorrow, and we'd make the most of it. So for the rest of the evening and long into the night, we talked about everything. The little things and the meaningful things. And we worked on the event I was planning for the next night at a place Drew suggested called Five Mile Stone. It would definitely be a night to remember.

CHAPTER 20

The following day, we had martinis and a few kisses at Drew's before the party. He looked smashing in a black suit, with a crisp white shirt and black and red tie. He seemed to think I looked pretty great in my slinky black, low back dress, with my hair up and a few curls coiling down here and there. And I loved my shoes. Black satin strappies with a rosette on the toe and an ankle strap. Surprisingly comfortable, too, which I quickly learned is a *must* in NYC. You just cannot have uncomfortable shoes. Ever.

We walked over to Five Mile Stone, a neighborhood bar and restaurant. Inside, the hostess took us upstairs. Everything looked amazing. Yes, it was only October, but earlier in the day we had decorated the upstairs for Christmas. Twinkling lights, red bows, and greenery were placed here and there. Tall tables for people to gather around were dotted throughout the room. We had to get creative with the greenery because the evergreen branches weren't available yet anywhere, but we'd found some green leafy thing with red berries that worked just fine. Jazzy Christmas songs by the Rat Pack played in the background. It was splendid. Just as we got a glass of wine at the bar, our friends started arriving.

Father Espinoza was, of course, the first to walk in. Well, he fairly ran in. Arms wide open, he picked me up like I was weightless. He squished the air right out of me, leaving me choking a little and Drew in near hysterics, trying to cover it up.

"This must be the famous Father Espinoza," Drew declared, shaking the man's hand heartily, giving me a moment to get my breath back and make sure my dress was still covering what it needed to cover.

They hit it off immediately, and Drew took him to the bar to get a drink. I looked at them both and thought fondly of the original story of St. Nick. I would have loved to meet Rebekkah and Stephen, and see their love and their family grow.

Next, in walked Billy, my drill sergeant friend who had told me all about Christmas tree history and of course, the story of Thomas and the first tree at Rockefeller center. Billy had brought his wife, a delicate woman with large green eyes. I went over and chatted for a moment and as I suggested they get a cocktail, Mrs. Foxmorten came in. My back had been to the steps, but her voice carries well. As everyone knows who's within 100 feet of her…

"JANE!!!!! JANE SMITH!!!!! I'm here!!!! Yoohoo!!!!" She startled Billy's wife and I could hear Billy chuckling. Oh yeah! He'd been the one to set me up with her. I squinted my eyes at him and I swear, his grin and the gleam in his eye was saying, "Better you than me!"

"Gosh, I think Mrs. Foxmorten is here," I said drolly.

I went over to the dear woman, still waving her scarf over her head like she was trying to signal a rescue plane. I helped her with her coat and drew her over to the appetizers she'd been eyeing. Poppy would've enjoyed an evening like this, I think. I could imagine her dancing with her father to the jazzy tunes.

Drew came over to introduce himself to Mrs. Foxmorten and put his hand on my lower back, pulling me a tiny bit closer. Right at that moment, up the stairs came – no, she *rose* – Lucy Langford. AKA Wonder Woman. Everyone's heads swiveled in her direction. I scrutinized Drew.

Certain that he could feel my eyes piercing into him, he

said, "She's really…"

I raised my eyebrows.

"Tall."

"Mm hm… She is. Tall," I said with my eyes half-closed.

I could feel him chuckling as he drew me close, and kissed my neck. Okay then.

I took his hand and we walked over to meet Lucy. She was very interested in all the people at the soirée. I of course reminisced about the story of Clement Clarke Moore and his Aunt Barton who had made his poem part of history. Somehow all these people from the past were sharing the night with us.

As I started to introduce Lucy to Mrs. Foxmorten – because I thought that would be fun to watch – in walked our final guests: Ho and Geoffrey. They must have met downstairs because they were in an animated discussion, obvious fast friends. Geoffrey was swinging his cane around with wild abandon, managing to get it hooked on one of the coats hung near him. Ho gently released it, but neither of them skipped a beat in whatever conversation they were thoroughly enjoying.

I walked over to them, bobbing and weaving to dodge Geoffrey's cane. Funnily enough, that old Daffy Duck cartoon popped into my head; the one where he's playing Robin Hood. Ho-haha-dodge-turn-parry-twist! I made it safely to them and gave them both a hug, thanking them for coming. Looking at Geoffrey, I could see Lou Buckley. I'd looked up Lou's photograph in some old archives, and Geoffrey definitely resembled him. The thought made me wish Lou, Virginia and Mr. Church could have been here with us.

And then, I almost dropped my wine glass. Up the stairs, in a brown suit, looking as average as ever but with a smile that was anything but... My brother Jim. "What!" I exclaimed as he ran up the final three stairs to scoop me up in a big hug. "What are you doing here?" I said as he swung me back and forth.

"Haha! I thought you'd be surprised! I got an interesting email from a friend of yours. I think a *new friend*..." He said in the tone only brothers use to tease their sisters, waggling his eyebrows at me.

"Cut it out, Jimmy," I said, playfully pushing him. My *new friend* chose that moment to walk up to us.

"Drew! Meet my brother, Jim. But it seems you've already met..." I said, shaking my head and grinning.

"Oh yes. We've had some delightful little emails back and forth," said Drew. What? "I thought he wouldn't want to miss out on this great idea of yours." He shook hands with Jim as he said, "I hear your dad's a meteorologist. That's really cool."

"Bah!" laughed Jim, turning toward me. "You told him that?"

Before I could answer, Drew said, "Yeah, she told me. Because I told her my name was Clompsburg. Just to mess with her."

"Ha ha ha!" laughed Jim. "I knew I liked you, Drew."

"Shut up Jimmy," I said.

Drew pulled me toward him as Jim decided to saunter over to Wonder Woman. Oh boy.

"That was a really sweet thing to do, Drew. Thank you."

"I know you love him. I figured, he might be the one to help us figure out how to segue between this new life of my Coco and the former life of Jane in Chicago."

"He just might be able to do that," I said. And don't think for a minute I missed the "my Coco" bit. That had a lovely ring to it.

After we all mingled a while, I could see many new friendships forming across the room. I nodded to Drew and then asked the bartender to bring down the music a little. I waved everyone over, to come a bit closer.

"I wanted to thank all of you for your help. These stories are your stories and it's been a privilege to hear your history and get a glimpse into the lives of some truly wonderful people. Every event, every celebration that has happened over the centuries to make Christmas what it is today, began with one person. One idea. And through courage, sometimes the hardest kind, such as forgiving oneself or taking a step toward reconciliation… Through unfettered joy and wonder, sometimes helping others to see it along the way… And through love, the kind that can span arguments, boredom (I smiled meaningfully at Drew), sadness, and even fear… we find the essence of what makes Christmas so special. This journey through an assignment that I originally *did not want*, has taught me so much and my life is richer for it. I, for one, will never see Christmas in quite the same way." As I was about to make a toast, I noticed two gentlemen in suits climb up the stairs to join us. I didn't recognize them, but I saw Drew make a little gesture toward them.

I raised my glass, "So here's a toast for us all. May your Christmas, and your lives, be touched by these friendships, these wonderful pieces of history, and what has quickly become my favorite city, New York! Cheers!" Sips and claps and cheers went all around the room.

But before the crowd dispersed into their own little conversations, Drew got everyone's attention. "I actually have something to say! Something unexpected happened as a result of Jane's work on this historic article. Together we were able to solve a family mystery that began during World War I. My great-grandfather was a soldier at the front when the spontaneous Christmas Truce of 1914 happened. He met a German that day, in No-Man's land, fully knowing that to step out there could mean death; and where consorting with the enemy was one step away from treason and the death penalty. But peace won that day. Even in the midst of hell.

"My family received a letter from him, but the first half of the letter has been missing for decades. Jane found the missing half of the letter. And through it, we were able to locate in a safe deposit box, a small package the German soldier handed to him on the battlefield. This is it."

He carefully handed the envelope with Franz Marc's sketchbook in it to the two gentlemen who had just arrived. Their faces had been wary and they looked uncertain as to why they'd been summoned to my Christmas party in October. But as Drew explained the story, their eyes grew intense with hope and profound interest.

The larger blond man opened the envelope, pulling out the sketchbook and then gingerly opening it. The whole upstairs room had gone completely silent except for a soft song playing in the background. We all stepped an inch closer, craning our necks to see their reaction to the book.

The tall, thin brunette man put his hand to his mouth and murmured with just a hint of a German accent, "Oh my God. It's his, isn't it?" The blond man nodded, unable to speak. As one, they both looked up at Drew and me, enormous smiles beaming on their previously solemn faces.

To everyone, Drew said, "These are two descendants of

the man whose sketchbook we found. The artist Franz Marc."

Lucy Langford, dearly loving history, almost came unglued. She wanted her hands on that book and looked as if she might faint or pee her pants at any second. Father Espinoza seemed to also know who Franz Marc was and shook his head marveling at the destiny of it all. Then I had to hold back a laugh as I heard Mrs. Foxmorten crow nice and loud over the crowd, "Who's Franz Marc?"

We turned the music back up, got more beer and wine, and had a great time. Later in the evening, some softer music was playing and I waved over at Father Espinoza to join me at a table in the corner, out of the way and a perfect place to ask a question that had been niggling at me.

He came over to the table, beer in hand, and sat down with me. "This is wonderful, Jane. I am so honored to be part of it all."

"It's really been a special week, hasn't it?" I said, feeling full and content. More so than I had ever felt.

"You look like you have a question on that lovely, curious face of yours," he commented, eyes glinting from the fairy lights strung behind me.

I smiled. "I do. You know… I'm a journalist. So I'm always on the hunt for good stories, mysteries to be solved, more information... And I feel like most of my life I've been searching for something. Like an important piece to a puzzle and I can never locate it. But this week… I don't know…" I said, shaking my head, still trying to figure it out. I felt like I had found something. But I couldn't put words to it, which was driving me crazy.

He nodded with understanding. I started to ask him my niggling question, "During this week of talking about

Christmas and traditions, why–"

"–Didn't I talk about the religious stuff?" he interrupted.

"Hah!" I laughed. "Yeah. I know all these traditions point to the reason for Christmas, the Christ child being born. But why haven't you talked about that?"

He smiled knowingly. "Oh I *have,* Jane."

I squinted at him, trying to figure out what he was saying, shaking my head a little.

"Here. Let me tell you a story. Maybe it will help you with your own story."

I sat back, grasped my red wine and prepared to enjoy a good story. I loved his stories.

He contemplated what he was going to say for a moment, then began. "Think of a dark, scary, lonely place. Think about not hearing from your loved ones, your family, for a very, very long time. So long in fact, you wonder if they forgot about you. It's cold. And you're very afraid. Death is all around you, and you can't imagine life getting any worse. All you want is a word. Just a word to know that you're not forgotten and that they'll tell you how to get home.

"Then imagine, just when you feel that you can't take one more tragedy, one more lonely night... You don't receive just a word, you see your very own father, riding a horse, carrying a golden light that promises goodness and safety. He comes to you. Not to tell you how to get home, but to *carry you home.* That is what Christmas is all about, Jane. God the Father didn't tell us how to behave properly to earn our way home, He came to get us Himself."

He bent closer to me, his voice full of wonder and his eyes twinkling. "All these stories you're pulling together of Saint Nicholas, Santa Claus, the Christmas tree... they all point to that colorful, beautiful, creative, over-the-top extravagance of God coming to us. I think we sometimes forget that God is full of color, laughter, whimsy, mystery, wonder, and a love that is bigger than we'll ever understand. *That* is why Christmas is important. It reminds us of that. So, Jane. You did hear all about the religious aspect of Christmas. You just didn't realize it was so cool."

I laughed out loud.

"Now, Jane dear. I hope that every Christmas, whether you are in a time of plenty or in want, whether you are sad or happy, whether you are lonely or your family is driving you crazy...will be a time for getting a glimpse of all that goodness. Cheers my dear." He stood up, tapped my wine glass with his bottle and walked off. Mission accomplished.

Now wasn't *that* something. I looked around the room, enjoying the sight of my new friends and a satisfied feeling of joy. I felt a hand on my shoulder.

"He's right, you know," said Jim.

"Hey! You were eavesdropping!" I accused, cracking up.

"Absolutely."

"You're incorrigible."

"It's my charm," said my funny brother as he sat down. "You look beautiful, Jane."

"Well thank you!"

"And it's not just the outside. I heard you tell the Father that you were looking for something. You look more content that you've ever looked before."

I nodded. "You know? I am. I'm still working on it, but I do feel like I found what I was looking for."

"I'm glad. Now let's go dance," he said, putting my glass down for me and taking my hand.

We did a fabulous little swing dance to *I've Got My Love*

to Keep Me Warm by Dean Martin. Well, he did a fabulous dance, I just tried to keep up and not break his toes by stepping on them. It was fun. After the song finished, *What Are You Doing New Year's Eve* came on and I felt a hand on my back.

"Can I cut in, Jim?" asked Drew.

"You bet!" said Jim, clapping Drew on the back.

He drew me by the hand, twirled me once making me laugh, then drew me nice and close. My left hand on his shoulder, my right clasped in his, curled up between us. We swayed back and forth to Harry Connick Jr. It was a song I'd always associate with this place, this city, this man.

"That was incredible, bringing the Franz Marc people here, Drew."

"It felt right. Poor Franz was only 36 when he was killed. He had so much promise. That sketchbook is priceless," he said thoughtfully. "My firm is working with their attorneys to make sure it's appraised properly and that the story of our two families becomes part of the museum piece. Honestly, I think its sentimental value exceeds the monetary value."

"I still wonder how Willow's letter came into my possession. I can't figure it out," I said.

"Sometimes... magic just happens," he whispered.

"Yeah. It does," I whispered back as he bent down and kissed me.

Chapter 21

Chicago, IL
November 2015

It was Thanksgiving Day. I was making a big dinner, full style points. Thank goodness my mother and father liked to celebrate as a family, not with the other millions of Americans on the actual day of Thanksgiving, but on the following Sunday. I'm not sure where that tradition began, but it really couldn't be more perfect. I get to make my own full-salt turkey, dressing, mashed potatoes (with flavor!), gravy, sweet potato soufflé with pecans, and pumpkin pie on the actual day. There is nothing more fun than making all those delectable dishes while the parades were running on the TV in the background.

I was happily cooking and preparing for all our friends coming over later to celebrate. The onions and celery were sizzling in the pan for the stuffing. The scent of the fresh herbs and butter rubbed onto the turkey and baking to yummy goodness floated throughout the house, along with the sweet and spicy smell of the sweet potatoes, brown sugar and cinnamon. Not to mention the best pumpkin pie. It was the kind made with sweetened condensed milk. It rocks. Far creamier and tastier than the kind with evaporated milk. Yum.

It was funny being back here in Chicago. My Christmas article was looking great. The poignant human interest stories were a big hit. But it was still weird. Drew and I talked a lot. But you know, long distance relationships are tough. I was thinking about my life in Chicago; I could feel that drowsiness again. And I didn't want to give in to it.

Something would have to be done. Drew had flown out to North Carolina to see his relatives for Thanksgiving, but we were planning on seeing each other over Christmas. No actual plans had been made, yet. I hoped a trip to New York would work out.

Just as I was thinking we might need a little more wine, and that I'd text my roommate Bianca to grab some on her way back from the gym, the doorbell rang. Shoot! She must have come back already.

I opened the door. And there was Drew. He was standing on the steps to our house.

"What!" I exclaimed, a huge smile plastered to my face.

"Hey, Coco," said Drew, grinning widely.

That's when I slammed the door shut.

Then I opened it. "I'm just kidding! Payback. Now get your butt in here!"

He laughed. "You still remember that, huh?" he said, running up the steps and putting his bags down. He swept me up and planted a kiss on me, his lips still cold from the wind outside, smelling of his good cologne and winter.

We wandered to the kitchen, the delicious smells coming from there pulling us both. I stirred a few things, peeked in at my turkey, and asked Drew what he'd like to do while he was in town.

"I'd love to go shopping along Michigan Avenue, of course," he said. "But, I really, really want to meet your Spidey editor. I've *got* to see him in person."

I laughed, "Sure! Wear your earplugs. I'll take you to my favorite coffee shop and lounge, too. You'll love The Library. Besides, my friends there haven't gotten their fill of harassing me for coming to love my Christmas assignment. They could use a few more days," I said with a smirk.

We caught up on the little things that are more fun to talk about in person than over the phone. Of course I heard about how his trip to see relatives in North Carolina had all been a ruse to surprise me. I asked about his current clients at work and he filled me in on the Franz Marc family. They invited us to Kochel am See, Germany to see the Franz Marc museum. They would be highlighting his sketchbook there and the interesting story involving Drew's family. After I tinkered around the kitchen; stirring, checking the cooking times, and adding a little more sugar to my cold apple, cranberry and orange slaw, we sat by the fire in my living room, drinking wine. It was divine.

"You know, you lied to me," I said, pulling my legs over onto his lap, scooching close.

"What do you mean?" he asked, smiling quizzically.

"When we sat in that Luncheonette on Third Avenue in New York, you told me you didn't like Christmas."

"Oh that's right! I did, didn't I?" He took a sip of wine and set his glass down. "You're right. I lied."

"You love Christmas, don't you?" I accused playfully.

"Yep! I was just trying to get you to lower your defenses. I figured you just hadn't gotten the chance to see the real deal yet."

"That's true. I think I did get a chance to really see it," I said thoughtfully. "And it has merit. Maybe."

"Maybe!" he said in mock outrage.

I laughed. "I think every story I wrote about showed a... I don't know... a supernatural aspect to the holiday. Especially Phillips Brooks."

"How so?" he asked, taking a drink of wine.

"I think I had been so stuck on the boring bits and feeling trapped, that I didn't know to be prepared for magic.

None of those people set out to change history, really, they were just going about their lives, being willing to dare to hope and dream – even in the midst of regular, average or even poor lives. In the process they created remarkable moments. And Brooks had been so heartbroken and depleted. Yet he found that magic even in the smallness of everyday things."

Drew smiled thoughtfully, and I suddenly remembered something. "Ooh! I have something to give you! I can't believe you showed up today. I just found it this morning. I'll be right back!" I ran over to the stairs and raced up, heart thumping, over to my desk, grasped the parcel, and ran back down.

I plopped down on the couch and laughed as I saw Drew urgently setting his glass down, realizing my re-entry was going to be rather rambunctious.

"Here you go," I said, with a seductive little whisper that piqued his curiosity. I was so excited.

He opened the manila envelope and carefully pulled out a large hard cover book inside. It wasn't very thick, and it had a small image on the front of a little snow-covered house, with Santa and his sleigh arriving in mid-air, about to land on the roof.

"*Twas' the Night Before Christmas*!" he exclaimed. "This is beautiful."

"Open it," I said, with a knowing tone of 'you ain't seen nuthin' yet.'

He opened the cover and saw the title on the inside, and then his eyes went to the left. There was something in script written there, faded from years gone by, but still legible.

"Read the inscription," I whispered into his ear, having come right up against him.

"You're distracting me," he said with his devilish grin.

"I know. Read it anyway."

He took a close look and read out loud, "Dearest Christina. Merriest of Christmases my dear girl. All my love, Aunt Willow. *Aunt Willow*?"

"I know!" I squeaked.

"Where did you get this?" he asked, baffled.

"This has to be where the half-letter to Willow fell from."

"What? How did you get it?" he asked, his hand brushing back his hair, both of us clearly wondering how this could've happened. Something far bigger than coincidence was at work.

"It was meant to be given to me from my editor's assistant, Moxie. But in the hustle to get me the information, she'd left it on her desk. I didn't see it until I went into the office yesterday. And I didn't notice the inscription until this morning when I decided to look through it. The letter must have been slipped inside somehow, and fallen out into the pile she did give me. I can't think of any other way."

"But how did it get from New York City to Chicago?"

"Look at the back cover."

He turned to the back and on the inside of the back cover were two stamps: one from a New York City children's bookstore and the second from the Chicago Public Library.

"Well I'll be," he said. "I do have a cousin named Christina. It must have been lost at some point and then donated to a library. I guess we discovered a little more of that Christmas magic."

"Yes, we did," I said. I took the book from his hands and set it on the table. I put my arms around his neck, arranging myself across his lap. "So... what *are* you doing New Years' Eve, Drew?" I asked. Instead of answering, as he held me in his arms, he slowly brought his lips down to mine.

He pulled away with a smile, and said, "Well, my dear Coco. I'm hoping to spend it with The Christmas Journalist."

I smiled, thinking that this was a great new beginning.

"Besides, I have an idea for your next Christmas article!"

Oh boy. I'm gonna' need some hot cocoa and fries...

THE END

The First Rockefeller Center Christmas Tree

New York City 1931

First Rockefeller Center Tree
Public Domain / Fair Use

The people in Chapter 5 are fictitious except of course the cameo of John D. Rockefeller, Jr. The first tree was set up by the construction workers in 1931 as Rockefeller Center was being built. I always wondered about that man – that first person – who thought a tree would be a good idea. Everyone has a backstory, and I hope that the story of Thomas Murphy gives you a glimpse into the real life of people living in New York City in the early 1930s.

Radio History

Brant Rock, Massachusetts 1906

Wireless station, Brant Rock, Massachusetts, 1906
Public Domain

Reginald Fessenden
Public Domain

I found an incredible document from the California Military History written by Lieutenant Frederick N. Freeman to relay the actual events that did occur in the aftermath of the earthquake of 1906. Reginald Fessenden was a renowned inventor, and he did face ridicule in his dreams of what the radio could really do. His work with the radio changed the history of the world.

Saint Nicholas

Myra, Turkey 351 A.D

There are many stories of significant miracles that Saint Nicholas performed. The story of the three daughters and Saint Nicholas' generous gift is the most prevalent. I took artistic license to consider how the events might have unfolded and I thought it would be interesting to consider that eldest daughter. Sometimes we make choices that we regret, it's in those times that grace can be hard to receive. But then again, when it is received, those moments become remarkable.

"Gentile da Fabriano 063" by Gentile da Fabriano
Public Domain

'Twas the Night Before Christmas

December, 1822 Clement Clarke Moore wrote the poem for his children and a year later his poem was submitted anonymously to the papers. It did have his name on it, but who exactly submitted it remains a mystery.

Clement Clarke Moore
Public Domain

"Merry Old Santa Claus"
January 1, 1881 edition of *Harper's Weekly*
Public Domain

Abraham Lincoln and Phillips Brooks

Phillips Brooks did indeed do all these things. And the Jewish Temple Shireath held that particular service for Abraham Lincoln. People of all backgrounds and faiths came together both to fight for freedom, and to mourn the loss of our great president. I found a fantastic article listed in the bibliography about that infamous day, and I highly recommend it as an illuminating read.

Phillips Brooks
Public Domain

The Funeral of President Lincoln,
New York, April 25th, 1865
New York Public Library Digital Collections
Public Domain

Virginia O'Hanlan, Mr. Church and Lou Buckley
New York City
September 20, 1897

Mr. Church and Virginia O'Hanlan were in fact both real people. Francis Church is the son of a Methodist minister and had a long career at *The Sun.* Lou Buckley is a nod to the real-life Sam Battle. Sam was indeed the first NYPD African American officer. He and his family did move from the south and he was school-age at the time that Church's editorial letter came out. Sam saved the life of another officer and was instrumental in many successful operations of the NYPD.

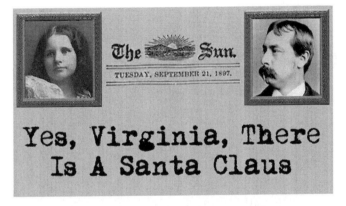

The Sun's Response to Virginia O'Hanlan
Photos Public Domain

Samuel J. Battle
Public Domain

The World War I Christmas Truce

The Christmas Truce of 1914 did happen. Over 150,000 troops took part in the spontaneous peace all along the Front in France. Franz Marc was in the German army at the time after he voluntarily joined in 1914, thinking that war would renew the European society. He was immediately sent to the front. He perished in the Battle of Verdun in 1916. The German government's release forms did not get to him in time. Despite having a decorated war record, the Nazis posthumously condemned him as a degenerate and removed 130 of his works from public collections. Later, it was

255

discovered that many of the declared "degenerate" works were looted by the Nazis.

"Christmas Truce 1914" by Robson Harold B
Public Domain

Christmas Truce Football Game
Public Domain

Franz Marc, 1910
The anthology The Unforgotten
Ernst Jünger 1928
Public Domain

Bibliography

Collins, Ace. *Stories Behind the Great Traditions of Christmas.* Michigan: Zondervan, September 29, 2003.

Hendrix, John. *Shooting the Stars.* New York: Harry N. Abrams, October 7, 2014.

Korn, Bertram W. *American Jewry and the Civil War.* Virginia: R. Bemis Pub Ltd., December 1, 1995

Lowe, David Garrard. *Art Deco New York.* New York: Watson-Guptill Publications, 2004.

McPherson, James M. *For Cause and Comrades: Why Men Fought in The Civil War.* Oxford: Oxford University Press, November 5, 1998.

Swanson, James L. *Blood Crimes: The Funeral of Abraham Lincoln and the Chase for Jefferson Davis.* New York: William Morrow Paperbacks, August 16, 2011.

Tolkein, J.R.R. *Letters From Father Christmas.* New York: Mariner Books, November 15, 2004.

1906 Culture and Earthquake

https://en.m.wikipedia.org/wiki/1906_in_the_United_States

http://californiamilitaryhistory.org/PerrySFEarthquake.html

http://www.ohio.edu/people/postr/mrt/Cmas1906.htm

Clement Clarke Moore

http://www.britannica.com/biography/Clement-Clarke-Moore